Heart of Ash

A Tryst Island Erotic Romance

SABRINA YORK

DEDICATION

This book is dedicated to Emily Cale, Tina Donahue and Sidney Bristol.
When you read the book, you'll know why, if you don't already.

ACKNOWLEDGEMENTS

First of all, thanks to my amazing beta readers, Charmaine Arredondo, Laurie A., Kim Brown, Carmen Cook, Shelly Estes, Angie Lane, Regina Ross and Michelle Wilson. And to my amazing street team who shares the word about my books: Crystal Biby, Kim Brown, Fedora Chen, Celeste Deveney, Shelly Estes, Stephanie Felix, Angie Lane, Rose Lipscomb, Laurie Peterson, Tina Reiter, Hollie Rieth, Regina Ross, Dee Thomas as well as Christy, Elf, Gaele and Laurie.

My deepest appreciation to Wicked Smart Designs for a gorgeous cover and to my editor Monica Britt for helping me whip this novella into shape. I bow deeply before Shelly Estes, who suggested the rockin' title.

Thank you so much to my dear author friends for your support: Emily Cale, Kristine Cayne, Dana Delamar, Cerise de Land, Delilah Devlin, Lisa Fox, Desiree Holt, and Tina Donahue.

To all my friends in the Greater Seattle Romance Writers of America, Passionate Ink and Rose City Romance Writers groups, thank you for all your support and encouragement.

CHAPTER ONE

Emily Donahue tipped her face into the breeze, enjoying the spray wafting up as the ferry sliced its way through the deep cool waters of Puget Sound. She stood at the bow, her favorite spot, holding back the urge to crow, "I'm the queen of the world!"

As much as she loved spending the weekend with her friends at the vacation house they shared on Tryst Island, she loved the ferry ride more.

There was something about water, the ocean, the slapping waves, that invigorated her, woke her up, made her feel alive. The view was spectacular. Emerald islands dotted the azure sea as far as the eye could see. The bird's egg blue sky was laced with fat white clouds. Rainbows sparkled as the sunshine danced over the water.

The boat jounced and a cool mist surrounded her. She licked her lips, tasting the salt, and laughed out loud.

Glorious. It was simply—

"Well, hello beautiful."

Irritation trickled through her as a low voice intruded on her reverie. Not because a voice intruded on her reverie, but because it was a man's voice.

She could just ignore him. If she'd been anyone else—her friend Bella, perhaps—she might have. But Emily had been born and bred to be a lady. And ladies were polite. Even to people who weren't.

It was a curse.

She steeled her spine and turned away from the glorious panoply to look at the man who had sidled up next to her. Her breath slowed. Her muscles tightened. She tried, very hard, not to grimace.

Grimacing was not polite in the least.

But it was difficult to maintain her expressionless mien. She knew his type. Disliked his type. Intensely.

1

Judging from his outfit and his smug, entitled smirk, he was a typical trust fund baby. So like all those boys she'd known in college. And the ring on his pinkie branded him as a frat boy. Or at least he had been once.

Some men never outgrew being a frat boy.

This frat boy was tall and bulky with an unruly mop of brown hair. He held a drink in a red plastic cup like this was some kind of kegger. His linen shirt, unbuttoned halfway to his navel, revealed a thick mat of dark curls. His ascot flapped in the wind. And yes, he wore an ascot. Worse than that, a hint of predatory interest glinted in his eyes.

He was the epitome of everything she disliked about men. And here she was. Trapped by him, cornered in the bow of the boat. She glanced around, a frantic hunt for one of her friends, but no. They were alone. Utterly alone.

She forced away the flicker of panic—panic served no purpose—and eased her fingers through her hair, casually unfastening her barrette. If push came to shove, she could gore him with it.

The boor leaned in, way too close. His breath wafted over her cheek in a bilious huff. She doubted one could get drunk from inhaling fumes, but the smell of alcohol emanating from him was overwhelming. As though he were steeped in it. Emily leaned back against the rail, disciplining herself not to gasp for fresh air. A dark cloud rose and roiled in her head.

"Did it hurt?" he asked.

Emily frowned. "D-did what hurt?"

"When you fell from heaven?"

All fear flew in the face of his absurdity. She gaped at him as his words hit home. Seriously? Her third grade class could come up with better pick-up lines. Although she hoped they never did.

Why, oh why, did she always seem to attract men like this? All she wanted was a nice, sweet man. Someone she could feel safe with. Someone who cherished her for who she was.

Not a horndog on the prowl for an easy lay.

Was that too much to ask?

The boat hit a swell and the horndog's drink sloshed all over her skirt. Emily didn't care, because this was a perfect excuse to flee. She swiped at the stain and murmured, "Oh no," and pushed past him with a pained smile and scuttled away. Not to scrub out the spot. Just to escape his leer.

He might have been a decent guy, if a little drunk, but it didn't matter. Something about him set her teeth on edge, and Emily had vowed never to ignore her gut again. Not when it came to men, especially men like *him*.

Relief flooded her when she spotted her friends at a table in the coffee shop on the ferry's upper deck. She slid into the open seat between Jamie and Kaitlin and gusted, "Douche alert." Bella had coined the term, one they all now used to warn the others of impending douchebaggery.

Kaitlin, bless her heart, took Emily's hand and gave it a soft squeeze, calming her. Kaitlin always knew how to calm her.

"Where?" Jamie crunched into a pastry. It crumbled to bits and flaked all over her t-shirt.

Emily winced. It was a damn shame to waste all those flakes. The bag on the table sported the Stud Muffin logo, so she knew it was one of Tara's evil creations. She was always creating evil, that Tara.

But it was a delicious kind of evil.

They were all delighted whenever Kristi invited Tara to spend the weekend on the island. Because she always brought a healthy supply of high-calorie sin.

Emily reached out and blotted the crumbs that fell on Jamie's plate. Pastries always soothed her, but she had to limit herself to crumbs because carbs had a tendency to collect around her waist. "Out on the deck. He's wearing an ascot."

Tara looked up from the papers she was studying and snorted. "Oh, holy hell. Him?"

Kaitlin rolled her eyes and pursed her lips. Even like that, with her eyes rolling and her lips pursed, she was beautiful. Kaitlin was a stunning redhead. Her face was perfection, her figure exquisite, like a woodland elf. Emily felt like a rhinoceros next to her. "That creep cornered me in the hall earlier. I had to spill my coffee on him to escape."

Emily nibbled her lower lip. "I was luckier. He spilled his drink on me." She showed them the stain, which had spread into the cherries printed on the fabric. Damn. She'd liked this skirt. It was cheerful and whimsical and made her feel happy. Now it was ruined.

She'd picked up this outfit at a thrift store. All her clothes came from thrift stores, much to her mother's chagrin. But she taught third grade. It wasn't practical to wear expensive clothes when one never knew what kind of grunge one might pick up in the course of the day. More often than not she came home with worms in her pocket.

Jamie bent and sniffed at the fabric. "What the hell was he drinking?" Her brown eyes narrowed. She sniffed again. "Vodka with cranberry juice? A squeeze of lime?" Jamie was something of a savant. Identifying someone's drink from nothing more than a whiff was one of her bar tricks. She made a fortune in quarters at Darby's on the weekends.

"Where'd he get vodka?" Tara asked. "I thought they didn't serve hard alcohol on ferries."

Just then, Ascot Man pushed into the room and joined two men seated in the far corner of the cafeteria. He upended a flask into his drink. "Apparently he brought his own," Jamie quipped.

"Goddamn frat boys." Kaitlin muttered. Though she cloaked it with a smile, there was a definite hint of bitterness in her tone. She and Emily exchanged a glance. A memory rose in Emily's mind. Two girls at a frat party. Lured to an isolated room…

She pushed the memory back into the shadows.

"Do you know them?" Jamie asked.

Kaitlin fiddled with her napkin. "Maybe. The handsome one went to the U."

Tara wrinkled her nose. "Which one's the handsome one?"

Emily blotted more crumbs. Yeah. They were all pretty cute, in a frat boy way. Except Ascot Man. He was just droopy.

"The one with the spiky hair."

Jamie leaned to the side. "Which one with the spiky hair? I swear. Those guys all look alike to me."

"The one with the dark hair. In office casual. I think his name is…Parker."

Something in Kaitlin's voice caught Emily's attention. Surreptitiously, she studied the frat boy with the spiky hair in office casual. He was definitely good looking, with a wide, handsome face and eyes that slanted a bit at the corners. And he did seem familiar.

The memory rose again. Unease trickled through her. She shifted in her seat. Blotted more crumbs, though there were hardly any left.

"I met him at a frat party once…" Kaitlin trailed off. Everyone waited for her to finish, everyone but Emily, who knew she wouldn't.

They didn't want to hear that story anyway. No one did.

"I just hope it's not a rowdy weekend," Tara muttered.

Just then a raucous cheer went up in the corner and the girls groaned in tandem. The frat boys had already started to party, and they hadn't even reached the island yet.

But then the horn tooted and the engines revved in a backwards thrum, and Emily knew they were almost at their destination. As she bent to gather her things, her gaze fell on Ascot Man.

Her stomach clenched as he waggled his tongue at her.

Oh lord.

She might just barf.

Friday night at Darby's Bar and Grill was crazy.

Ash Bristol stepped from the sunshine into the shadowed tavern and glanced around at the milling crowd. He spotted an empty table and made his way toward it. His step faltered when he saw Bella Cross, but he just kept going.

Damn, she was hot. Long black hair, boobs out to here, a tiny nipped waist… But there was one thing he found very unattractive about her—the muscular arm draped over her shoulder. As hot as she was, Bella was dating Holt Lamm now. Any guy in his right mind would steer clear of those fists.

So even though his friend Cam, who was sitting with them, waved, Ash pretended not to notice and headed for an empty table like it was a door floating in the middle of the frigid, iceberg-speckled Atlantic.

His buddies were coming in on the six p.m. ferry and, after dropping their crap at the house, they'd be coming here. He checked his watch, the ostentatious Rolex his mother had given him on the illustrious occasion of his "first divorce." And yeah, the guys would be here any minute.

He hated wearing expensive shit. It was like crack for the gold diggers. But Mom expected him to wear it, so he did.

Darby's waitress, Charmaine, came by and handed him a menu. "Just one?" she asked, flicking her platinum blond hair, cut in an asymmetrical bob. Normally, asymmetrical anything set his teeth on edge, but Charmaine pulled it off.

"There will be four of us. Could I get a beer?"

"Sure thing, sweetie," she chirped. He watched as she sashayed away, enjoying the view. She was a honey, but she didn't fool Ash for a minute. If he got out of line, she'd use one of those steak knives in the silverware packet to slice off his nuts. Most of the regulars knew better than to get out of line. A guy who smacked Charmaine on the ass might just find a pot of scalding coffee pooling in his lap.

A burst of commotion at the door caught his attention and he grimaced. His friend Richie staggered in, raising his arms and bellowing, "Ladies, the real men have arrived." Silence settled on the bar as heads turned, but just as quickly as it had ceased, conversation resumed.

Apparently the ladies weren't all that impressed with the "real men."

Ash raised a hand motioning them over. He could tell right away Richie was drunk off his ass, and Devlin and Parker had been drinking too. He divined this when Parker nearly missed his seat and almost landed on the floor.

Great. It was going to be one of *those* weekends.

He motioned to Charmaine. When she made her way over to the table, he said, "Better get some food in these guys. Four burgers?"

"Bacon burgers," Richie said, way too loud.

"Bacon cheese burgers." Devlin added. Although he said this with a respectful smile in Charmaine's direction. And even added, "Pretty please." Devlin had known the pain of coffee-lap.

As she took the menus, she blew out a sigh and nodded. "Coming right up."

"Don't forget the fries," Richie commanded through a hiccup. As if she would. She might spit on them, though. If he didn't reel it in.

Richie, who'd been his friend since prep school, was kind of an ass and always had been. They'd been drinking buddies forever, so Ash tolerated his shit, but it was getting harder and harder. It seemed as though Ash, and

Parker and Devlin for that matter, were growing up, while Richie remained locked in emotional puberty.

Parker and Devlin though? Solid. He was pretty lucky to have guys like them in his corner.

Drunk or not.

Parker stiffened at his side. "Oh shit," he breathed. "There she is."

Ash glanced up to see who *she* was and his heart stalled. Holy hell. An angel had just stepped into Darby's. A beautiful girl with soft blonde curls and wide eyes. He couldn't see the color from here, but it hardly mattered. She was a delightful package and a punch to his solar plexus.

"Oh, baby. She is fine. I talked her up on the ferry. " Richie put out his chest. "She wants me."

Annoyance burned in Ash's gut. Why, he didn't know. She wasn't *his* angel. She was simply an angel. If she wanted Richie, she could have him.

No more relationships for Ash. No more blind trust. No more expectations.

"God, she's so fucking hot." Was Richie still talking? "I do dig a redhead," he added.

Ash blinked. A redhead? He scanned the group of women who had entered with his angel, the group now heading over to Cam's table—damn, he should have responded to that wave—and yes, there was a redhead. And a brunette with sixties-bangs and another girl with long jet-black hair pulled back in a ponytail. He'd hadn't noticed any of them.

His attention skewed back to the blonde. She smiled at something Cam said and a hot, hard arousal shot through him like a jagged bolt of lightning. God. That smile.

He really should have responded to Cam's wave.

At some point this weekend, he was going to have to meet that girl.

He'd sworn off relationships, but he sure as shit hadn't sworn off fucking. And she looked like she'd be a wild ride.

"Okay. I could tap that."

Ash blinked as someone voiced the words winging around in his head. He gaped at Devlin. Dev must be pretty drunk. He was usually a complete gentleman when it came to the ladies. "The redhead?"

"Whaa?" He didn't seem to be able to complete the word. "No. The hottie with the ponytail."

"I could so yank on that ponytail." Was Richie drooling? Awesome. At least he remembered to wipe his lip on his sleeve.

Ash grimaced. He was definitely the "designated walker" tonight. He hated babysitting.

Devlin glared at Richie who was leering at the brunette. "Hey. Ponytail is mine. I called it." He attempted to punch Richie on the shoulder but he missed and punched the chair instead. "Ow."

It was all Ash could do not to roll his eyes. "No fighting boys."

Parker grinned. "There are plenty of babes to go around."

"But they're all at the other table." Richie leaned in and hissed, "We should go over there and steal them. Those two guys look like peckerwoods."

Ash cleared his throat. "That's Cam Jackson. And the big guy? The one with all the muscles? Holt Lamm."

"Holt Lamm?" Richie squeaked. "Shit."

"Who are they?" Devlin asked.

"They're friends of Lane's."

Richie studied the table across the room. "Which one is the cunt who cleaned him out?"

Ash winced at the use of that word. Especially in reference to Lucy, Lane's ex-wife. Who was a friend of his sister's. His fingers tightened. He didn't want to pound Richie into a pulp, but he would. He opened his mouth to respond, but Devlin beat him to it.

"Watch it McCleary." Last names were a bad sign, and Devlin's tone— lethal. Richie jerked to attention.

Parker frowned as well. "Lucy's a nice girl. And their divorce was animac… aminaca… friendly. Besides. Lucy didn't clean him out. She comes from money."

Dev snorted. "Not as much money as Lane."

"No one has as much money as Lane Daniels," Richie sneered, and then they all looked at Ash. Because they knew it wasn't true.

Ash didn't respond. Sure, his family had a lot of money, but it wasn't *his* money. He lived off an inheritance his grandfather had bequeathed to him. He'd never made a dime in his life. Besides, he could care less about the fucking money. The money was an albatross around his neck. It made him a target. Attracted the worst kind of women.

He upended his beer.

"Still…" Richie leaned back so Charmaine could set his plate before him. He almost leaned too far and wobbled for balance. Once he recovered himself, he continued. "The bitch got a bundle in the divorce." His gaze narrowed on Ash, who forced his features into a mask. He knew what was coming. "Like your bitch. Don't tell me you *like* that she got a fat settlement?"

Bile rose in his throat. Ash unrolled his silverware and set his napkin in his lap. He arranged the knife and fork and spoon in an orderly array before him.

"Serves you right. Guys like you and Lane Daniels should never get married," Richie continued, rocking back in his chair. "You should just pay for poontang. No messy divorce. No lawyers. No fuckin' golden payday for a cunt."

Ash couldn't help it. His foot shot out and knocked the leg of Richie's chair. The ass went sprawling back and landed on the floor with a thud. The other guys howled, but Ash did not.

The pain of his divorce was far too raw to have it bandied about in a bar. Jillian had used him. Seduced him, told him she fucking loved him, and then, once the "I dos" were said, the truth came out.

It was all about the money.

She'd said as much.

To his face.

Spat it, in fact.

It had been a shock. A complete shock. Because the viperous harpy he'd encountered in that honeymoon suite—after the marriage had been consummated, of course—had been diametrically opposed to the sweet, amiable woman he'd fallen for.

She'd played him all along.

And then laughed about it.

Laughed.

He'd resolved, then and there, never to give anyone such power over him again. His heart had burned out that night, burned to a crisp. He doubted he would ever recover. His heart would not magically heal and rise like the Phoenix from the ashes. He was done.

"Are you okay?" Parker asked, and Ash realized he'd bent his fork nearly in half.

He dropped it on the table and raked his fingers through his hair. "I'm fine." But he wasn't.

Because Ash Bristol, son of billionaire coffee magnate Adam Bristol and publishing heiress Mia Bristol-Finnerman-Cox, could never have the one thing he craved more than anything in the world.

A woman who loved him for himself.

It was stupid even to think about it.

So he didn't. And he ignored the deep dark chasm inside of him.

Or tried to.

CHAPTER TWO

Emily noticed *him* the minute she walked into the bar. In fact, she'd nearly tripped over the threshold because his beauty blinded her. It was silly to be so fanciful, but with his golden hair and muscles stretching his linen shirt, the lights behind forming a halo around him, he seemed like a God, stepped down from Olympus.

She'd never met a man who captured her interest like this. A man she could stare at until the end of time. But this guy did just that. There was something about him, something beyond his physical perfection, something that *spoke* to her.

She'd always had this fantasy that one day her Prince Charming would waltz into her life and she would just *know* he was the one. But none of the men she'd ever met had even come close to her ideal. She'd never had *that* feeling. She'd never set eyes on a man and thought, *Yep. That's him.*

Jamie joked she'd read too many fairy tales as a child, and Tara insisted it was too many romances, but Bella held there wasn't much difference between the two fantasies. Kaitlin simply advised that she not hold out for a Prince.

Regardless of her friend's advice, Emily was starting to doubt she could truly be interested in any man. At least, enough to risk being with him. In *that* way. Maybe she'd waited too long. Maybe, after what had happened, the fear, the walls were too great to breach.

That's why, when she saw *him*, and her pulse thrummed and her soul sang, her reaction surprised her so much. His presence hit her on a visceral level. It took an effort to turn away.

But not before she noticed he was sitting with the douche from the boat.

Pity, that.

"Oh, there's Cam." Kaitlin waved and hooked her arm in Emily's and they headed to the table in the center of the room where Kristi and Cam sat with Bella and Holt.

Emily's gaze stalled. Was that Holt's arm around Bella's shoulders?

She shot her friend a googley look and Bella responded with a smug grin. Heavens.

She'd always suspected Bella had a thing for Holt, but Emily never expected *this*. Not the way they fought like cats and dogs. She shot a glance at Kaitlin and whispered, "Did you see this coming?"

Kaitlin's only response was a small smile, but Emily could tell from her expression, she had, indeed, seen this coming.

Then again, Kaitlin saw just about everything coming.

They all took their seats and opened their menus and studied them diligently. And then, when Charmaine came by, ordered the same things they always ordered.

As they waited for their food, they chatted and got caught up. The biggest news was the two new couples that had formed within their long-standing group of friends. But no one mentioned that.

With the exception of Lane and Lucy, who had married in college and just recently divorced, none of the Dawgs, as they called themselves, had ever dated. Theirs had been a fierce camaraderie, formed in the dorms during an epic football season and enhanced when they all shared a house during their junior and senior years in college. There had been crushes and flirtations—even now, Drew was more than a little in love with Kaitlin—but no romantic hook ups had formed.

The guys in the group were like brothers. The girls like sisters.

So it was a bit awkward to see Cam and Kristi, and now Bella and Holt canoodling.

Then again, it was kind of sweet.

Kristi and Bella deserved to be happy.

And goodness, they looked happy.

Emily swallowed a lump of envy and focused her attention on her water glass, but found her gaze drifted with annoying regularity over to the table across the room. She let herself peek, every once in a while, just to memorize his features for her future fantasies. Because she'd never meet him. And if she did, she'd probably be far too intimidated to talk to him.

She didn't have any trouble talking to men about her fundraising causes, and certainly had no trouble counseling the fathers of her students or talking to her male friends. But a man this attractive? The walls shot up, her armor bristled and her tongue became impossibly tied.

Exasperation bubbled in her belly. She longed to be a free spirit, like Bella or Tara, unfettered by fear, uninhibited, willing to take a risk. But she wasn't.

Damn it. It had been years. She should be over it by now.

If only she could wave a magic wand. Become someone else, someone bold, intrepid, brave, for a while.

A man like that would be worth the risk.

Wouldn't he?

"Jesus," Kaitlin muttered as Ascot Man leaned back in his chair and went toppling into the sawdust. A cheer went up around the bar and Emily swallowed a guffaw. He'd scared her on the boat, looming over her, boxing her in, reminding her of another man. He wasn't so terribly daunting sprawled on the floor with peanut shells in his hair. The flare of satisfaction, seeing him humiliated like that, was probably beneath her.

"Who are those guys?" Tara asked.

Holt glanced over his shoulder. "The blond is Ash Bristol. He has the place next to ours."

Emily's ears perked up at that. She peeped over at her Greek God. *Ash.* His name was Ash.

And then she stilled. "Bristol?" she asked through numb lips. "As in the Bristol Foundation?"

Cam nodded. "Ash is the heir apparent."

Emily studied Ash's features from beneath veiled lashes and saw it. The family likeness. She'd worked many fundraising events with Adam Bristol, the CEO of Bristol Coffee Company, one of Seattle's most successful roasters. Adam, who was her father's age, was a wonderful man who cared deeply about many of the causes Emily championed.

If Ash were anything like his father…

Her heart gave a little flip.

Cam took a sip of his beer. "Ash is a friend of Lane's," he added, as though that explained everything. But then, it kind of did. Trust fund babies stuck together.

"And the others?" Tara asked.

Cam smirked. "I don't know the guy in the ascot." Snorts around the table at that. "But that's Parker Rieth in the blue and Devlin Fox in the Polo shirt."

Tara gasped. "That's *Devlin Fox?*"

All heads swung in her direction, probably because of the vitriol dripping from her tone. Emily had never heard Tara snarl, not quite like this.

"You know him?" Bella asked.

"He writes a Foodie Blog." This Tara spat as though it tasted bad. "He gave Stud Muffin a bad review."

"What?" A howl of dissension rose. No one dissed a Dawg and got away with it.

"Why the hell did he do that?" Holt grumbled. Tara's bakery was the hottest pastry shop in Seattle.

"Because I don't have gluten free." She crossed her arms over her chest and glared at the table across the room. And then muttered, "Big baby."

"They're all drunk as skunks." Bella wrinkled her nose, which was funny, because Bella knew her way around a bar pretty well.

Jamie blew out a breath. Her bangs fluffed up. "Looks like it's frat-central next door this weekend, ladies."

Tara set her chin. "We should make a pact."

"A pact?"

Holt and Cam, knowing what was coming, groaned.

"A pact to avoid them." Tara thrust her fist out to the center of the table and all the women piled their hands on top.

"To avoid the douche bags," they chorused.

Tara whipped her fist up in the air, sending all their hands flying. "Like the fucking plague."

It was a Girl Dawg pact.

Immutable and carved in stone.

A hint of regret wafted through Emily like a wraith, though she knew, even if there were no pact, she'd never have the courage to talk to a man like Ash.

Not ever.

And it annoyed the hell out of her.

"Hey."

Emily jumped. So focused on the starfish in the tide pool, she hadn't heard anyone approach. She turned, shaded her eyes from the sun and froze.

It was him.

The Greek God.

Again, wreathed by a brilliant halo.

What was it with this guy and halos?

Her friends constantly told her she was whimsical and fey, and maybe she was. But was it naïve to think it could be an omen?

Probably.

But for some reason, she couldn't squash the hope swelling in her breast.

"H-hey." Her pulse surged. Panic…and something else whipped through her. She tried to calm her roiling emotions. He was here. Talking to her. The very thing she'd been fantasizing about all evening. It took an effort to ignore her primal response. To stay put. But somehow she dredged up a modicum of courage and didn't leap to her feet and run away. She even managed a smile.

He hunkered down beside her and the flutter became a full boil. "What are you doing?"

She fixated on the little puddle of life, abandoned when the tide rushed off to occupy itself with more interesting pursuits, and shrugged. "J-just looking."

"Do you stare at water often?"

Emily blinked. She fought down an incongruous snort of laughter, but it escaped anyway. Before she could stop herself, she glanced at him. He was close. So close she could see the golden tinge of his lashes, the slight stubble on his cheeks, the tiny creases at the corner of his eyes.

His lips quirked, a crooked grin. She liked the way he grinned, though from the lines on his face, she suspected he was more often frowning.

"I…Whenever I can." She stood and brushed the damp sand from her knees and picked up her wide-brimmed hat. He stood too. Her breath stalled. Because he was tall. Way tall.

Big men made her especially nervous. How odd she didn't feel that right now. No. This wasn't fear. It was…something else entirely.

"I'm Ash." He thrust out a hand.

Her stomach clenched. He expected her to take it. To touch him. Touch *him*.

She reminded herself it was only a handshake. Nothing more. She reminded herself she was safe. And, indeed, a sudden *comfort* flooded her. She felt, deep in her soul, as if she knew him.

As though her soul recognized his.

Yep. He's the one.

Exhilaration swept through her, eroding long-held fears. A delicious lightness enrobed her.

Emily believed in trusting her instincts. And her instincts screamed he was someone special. Someone safe.

Of its own volition, her hand met his.

Electricity sizzled up her arm as their palms touched. Caressed. An unexpected and unfamiliar audaciousness settled over her. She met his gaze.

He stiffened. His pupils dilated. They stared at each other. It was probably her imagination that he felt the same simmering recognition.

"I'm Emily," she said, her voice sounding oddly coquettish to her ears.

"How do you do, Emily?" That reluctant grin again. Like he was apologizing for smiling.

"I do very well, Ash. Thank you." She nibbled her lip to hold back a grin of her own. She'd spent hours in elocution classes as a child, parroting these very words back to her tutor. Her mother had been diligent in training her daughters on every element of propriety. At that thought, she put on her floppy hat. Though it was early evening, the sun still beat down. It wouldn't do to freckle.

"Would you care to promenade?" he asked with a wink, playing along.

With his upbringing, he'd probably suffered through the same lessons.

She curtseyed. "I'd be delighted."

He thrust out an elbow.

Oh dear. He meant for her to take his arm.

She did, of course. It was the *polite* thing to do. It didn't hurt that his muscles were firm. They flexed beneath her fingers. And he was warm. She imagined she could feel his warmth seeping into her, melting the ice that had encased her heart since…

No. She wouldn't think about that.

But she was being fanciful again. This was only a stroll. Nothing more.

She cleared her throat, searching for a topic as they started down the beach toward the point. It was a beautiful summer evening. A cool, soothing breeze drifted off the water, riffling the needles of the fragrant pine trees standing sentinel along the shore. She set her hand on the top of her hat and tipped her face up to the sun.

"So, Ash, do you come here often?"

"That's supposed to be my line," he chuckled.

"A thousand pardons, sir."

"I do, though. As often as I can," he said. "How about you?"

She shrugged. "Now and then. When I can get away." Even though school was out, her calendar overflowed with commitments to the shelter and the food bank and the tutoring she did at Teen Waystation.

Those kinds of activities gave her mother conniptions. But Emily found it satisfying, helping people who really needed it. If her mother had her way, Emily would spend her days dressed like a poodle, tottering around a garden party eating finger sandwiches and bemoaning the lack of Perrier in Bangladesh.

"Busy life?"

She didn't quite understand his odd tone, but pressed the ping of uneasiness away. "Mmm. Very busy."

"Ah. Demanding boyfriend?"

"N-no. No boyfriend."

"Husband?"

"No husband."

"Dog?"

She threw back her head and laughed. "I do have a dog." Six actually, but three were rescues she was fostering. She'd probably keep them. "And cats."

"Ah. A menagerie."

"I love animals."

She smiled at him and his step faltered. His gaze flicked over her features and settled on her mouth. She licked her lips; it was a purely instinctual response to having one's lips stared at. She did not expect his nostrils to flare quite like that.

She knew he was thinking about kissing her. Just knew. Excitement rippled through her.

Oddly, there was no panic at the thought.

Just excitement.

Perhaps he was the one.

"So… What do you do, Emily of the Tide Pool?" The words were soft and slow, almost a seduction.

"I'm a teacher."

The muscles around his eyes tightened, infinitesimally. "A teacher."

"Mmm hmm." They rounded the point and the smaller companion island to the west came into view. They headed toward it.

An eagle soared overhead and she stopped in her tracks to watch. "Oh heavens," she breathed. "How magnificent." She turned to find his gaze riveted on her face. His intensity sent a ripple of nervousness through her. "An eagle," she said, in case he'd missed it. "It flew over to the other island." She pointed. In case he didn't know where the island was. Also, so he'd look. Over there. His avid attention on her mouth was making her restless.

Obligingly, he looked. "I think there's a convocation nesting there."

Emily blinked. "A what?"

"A convocation. It's what you call a group of eagles."

"It is?"

"Mmm hmm. A gaggle of geese. A murder of crows. A charm of hummingbirds. A convocation of eagles."

"A charm of hummingbirds? I rather like that. How do you know all this?"

He stubbed the sand with his toe. "I had a poster on my wall when I was a kid. I used to lie on the bed when no one was home and read it."

"When no one was home?"

His smile faded. He shoved his hands in his pockets. "There are lots of birds on the other island. I think they flock over there because there are fewer disruptions from humans." He shot her a glance. "Have you ever been there?"

"Oh no. It's private property."

"Yes, it is." A wicked glint appeared in his eye. "Would you like to trespass?"

"We couldn't." She returned her attention to the island as another eagle joined the first. They rose and drifted on the updrafts and circled each other like lovers. "It's so far."

"I can take you for a ride on my Jet Ski. We'll just zip over and I can show you where they nest, and then we'll come back."

"Y-you have a Jet Ski? I've never been on one."

He gaped. "Never?"

"Never."

"Emily of the Tide Pools, who loves staring at water, has never been on a Jet Ski? That seals it. You have to come."

"But won't the owner be angry?"

"No one lives there. There's a cabin, but no one lives there." He gave her an enticing grin. "Come on. You know you want to."

It wasn't the prospect of visiting a forbidden island that set her pulse pounding. It was going there with *him*. On a Jet Ski. Exhilaration whipped through her at the thought of sitting behind him, plastered against him. Wrapping her arms around his waist.

"Okay," she said. She had no idea why she said yes. No idea why the word came so easily. No idea why her spirit took flight. Maybe because this was one step—a tiny step but a step nonetheless—toward taking back her life. Reclaiming herself from the fear that had chained her for so long.

He smiled at her and, for the first time since they'd met, his smile was absolutely, unequivocally genuine.

CHAPTER THREE

Excellent.
Fucking excellent.
Like a lamb to slaughter.

Ash glanced up at the sky and gauged the color on the horizon. Just starting to show a hint of darkness. He took Emily's arm and led her back down the beach, past her house, hoping to hell no one saw them. If anyone stopped them, his plans would be for shit.

No one did.

All the guys at his place were sleeping off their buzzes, and he'd already prepped the Jet Ski and had it tied to the dock, so all he had to do was climb on and help her settle in behind him. "You might want to leave your hat," he said.

She tipped it off, letting it hang down her back. "It's my favorite hat."

"Okay." *Whatthefuckever.* "Put your arms around my waist," he said over his shoulder, willing his voice not to crack. But Jesus, when she did it, he nearly lost it. Her breasts pressed against his back and it made him dizzy. Because all the blood shot to his cock. He turned the key and revved the engine. "Hold on."

"Won't we get wet?" she called into his ear.

"Only a little." A lie. But a necessary one.

She squealed and clutched him as the craft lurched into motion and water splashed over her feet. He bit back a grin and patted her hands, tightly clasped, as they were, around his middle.

"It's okay," he yelled. "Just hang on tight."

And she did. Bless her. She clung to him like a limpet, molding her body against his, her crotch plastered against this ass. He tried not to think about that, because he didn't want to steer into the reef.

He'd made this trip a hundred times while he and Parker were building the cabin. He knew every rock, every swell, every wind pocket. He steeled himself as they rounded the point—it always gusted here—and when the blast hit, she clenched him harder.

Oh yeah. He couldn't wait to feel another clench…

Again, he had to discipline himself to focus on steering. Thinking about anything else could lead to disaster.

They reached the small island in no time and he reversed the engines as they floated toward the dock. It wasn't much of a dock, but it didn't need to be.

He grabbed the tether and pulled the boat in, then helped her off, cutting the engine and flipping a few key switches. She laughed as she shook out her pant legs. They were soaked to her knees.

There should be absolutely nothing sexy about a woman in purple overalls, flip-flops and a droopy hat. But when she laughed like that, like there was no greater joy in the world than being here, and when she gazed at him with her eyes wide and her lips slightly parted… Ash had never seen anything sexier in his life.

It poleaxed him.

A niggle of guilt speared him, for lying to her, for luring her, for the seduction he planned to unleash, but he thrust it away. She was a grownup. She'd come willingly.

And he wanted her.

And she wanted him.

He was certain of it.

"Come on." He took her hand and led her off the dock and onto the beach. "The nests are over here."

"Ooh. It's so pretty," she said as they headed down the shadowed path into the woods toward the nesting site. Or where it might possibly be. He hardly gave a shit.

"Mmm hmm."

"I love when the trees form a canopy like this. It's like a cathedral. See how the sun filters through in shafts?"

Damn, she was a chatterbox. "Mmm hmm."

"Oh look. Isn't that beautiful?"

He glanced to the left, where she was motioning. "The…spider's web?"

"Oh yes," she said. Now that she mentioned it, it was rather stunning. Geometric perfection dotted with glittering raindrops from a recent shower.

But seriously? He'd never met a woman who'd liked spider webs.

Her observations continued on, unabated, as they made their way through the woods. She loved the way the moss felted the branches, the way the sky peeked through the lacy leaves, the smell of the loam. Ash let her monologue wash over him, and occupied his mind with thoughts of silencing her…with a kiss.

18

"So what do you do, Ash?" she gusted, as they topped a rise.

"Hmm?"

"What do you do?"

For a living? Nothing. But he couldn't say that. "I like to play with glass." It was his passion. His only passion, anymore.

Something lit in her expression. Something he liked. A lot. She was pretty before. Now she was downright gorgeous. "Leaded or fused?"

A trickle of satisfaction dribbled through him. She knew. She knew the art. The one thing that gave his life some meaning. "Both. But I like fusing the most. I have a kiln."

"Really? Which kind?"

He named a model that made her murmur, "Nice."

Naturally. It was top of the fucking line. His whole life was top of the line.

Judging from her well-worn outfit, an obvious hand-me-down, she came from a very different background. Not that he cared. It hardly mattered. He didn't have marriage, or a relationship of any kind, in mind.

"Oh, I see them!" she cried.

Ash blinked and then followed her gaze. Holy hell. He hadn't been full of shit. At least, not completely. Several eagles perched on the treetops, ruffling their wings and scanning the woods.

"They're splendid." A sigh. "Just splendid."

Damn. Once he looked at her, he couldn't look away. She was so goddamn pretty to begin with, but with delight dancing in those wide eyes, she was irresistible. And damn, those eyes. They were an icy blue, ringed with an almost purple hue. Combined with her dark pupils, they were mesmerizing.

He couldn't resist. Couldn't wait a moment longer. He had to kiss her. Now.

He tipped up her face and came in slowly, giving her a chance to resist, step away, stop him.

She did not.

Her lips parted. Her tongue peeped out. A shudder walked through him.

Damn.

Damn. Damn.

His lips touched hers. Just a soft brush. A skim. A tantalizing tease. He tasted, smelled, felt wonderful.

Emily was typically very nervous around men, especially hunky and handsome men who seemed too self-assured for their own good. But something about Ash set her at ease. His smile, his laugh, his slightly reserved approach. She wasn't quite sure what it was, but she liked him.

Trusted him.

And this tender exploration was far too sweet. She didn't want it to end.

So she cupped his nape, went up on her tiptoes and opened her mouth against his.

His breath hitched, tangling with hers and, issuing a low growl in the back of his throat, he yanked her against him.

Holy Hannah, he was hard. His chest. His ropy, muscular arms…his groin. A scalding blush crept up her cheeks as she realized exactly what that firm pressure bespoke. Arousal. For her.

Normally, in a situation like this, when a man rubbed an erection against her like that, her natural reticence would kick in. Fear would flare. She'd back away. Fight free if necessary.

But no fear flared as Ash deepened the kiss. No nasty memories awoke. Anxiety did not claw at her bowels.

No. A joy, an elation unlike anything she'd ever experienced in a man's arms, flooded her.

Perhaps it was because she really, really liked this man. Or perhaps it was because, even though the kiss was wild and savage, he held her gently, as though she were a delicate China doll. As though he would let her go if she but asked.

Or perhaps it was simply because everything about this felt right.

Ash lifted his head and gazed down at her, a muscle working in his cheek. Slowly he released her, though his caress lingered as it slid away. "We—" He cleared his throat. "We should be getting back."

Her belly plunged. "Getting back?"

He looked up at the sky and for the first time, she realized dusk was falling. Ribbons of crimson and amber streaked through the puffy clouds. "Come on." He laced his fingers through hers and led her back to the dock. He stumbled a few times on upturned roots, because he wasn't watching where he was going. He was gazing at her.

Heat crawled up her neck.

He was so handsome. His hair was blond and sun-streaked. His face was broad, open, tan. His muscles bulged against the fabric of his shirt. Where they intertwined, her fingers tingled. He was perfect. Absolutely perfect.

They reached the dock way too soon and he released her hand to unlash the Jet Ski. "Do you want to drive back?" he asked.

"I couldn't."

"Sure you can. It's easy. I'll show you." He helped her onto the seat, in front, and then settled behind her. She leaned against him as the little craft bobbed in the waves. His warmth surrounded her. She shivered. "Just turn the key," he said, "and gun the throttle." She did. The engine revved. Then coughed. Then died.

She pursed her lips. "I think I did it wrong."

"Try again." His breath, fragrant and sweet, caressed her cheek.

She swallowed and focused and did it again.

And again, the engine died.

"Huh," he grunted. "Let me try."

His hands, long-fingered and sure, fiddled with the controls. The engine sputtered, but didn't catch. He sighed. "I think we might have flooded it."

It was getting dark. She glanced at him over her shoulder. "What do we do?"

"There's nothing we can do. But wait."

She shuddered. The thought of driving across the expanse of water to the main island in the dark was frightening.

He shrugged. "I guess we could spend the night here."

She froze. Apprehension rose. Or maybe it wasn't apprehension. Maybe it was anticipation. "Sp-spend the night?"

"We won't have to camp." He gave a little laugh. "There's a cabin."

"B-but my friends will be worried."

"Did you bring your cell phone? We can call them."

"No. Did you bring yours?"

He shook his head.

Emily gazed at the main island. It seemed so close, yet so far away.

Ash got off the Jet Ski and re-tied it to the dock, then settled a somber look on her. "I don't think we have any option, Em."

Normally, she didn't like nicknames, but she liked when he said it.

He reached out a hand and she took it, let him help her back onto the dock. He wrapped his arm around her shoulder and tugged her close. "Don't worry," he said. "It'll be okay."

And she believed him.

CHAPTER FOUR

The cabin was adorable, nestled as it was in the trees. It was a tiny one-story, but had a lovely porch that hung over the cliff, looking out on the water.

"There's no power," Ash said as he pushed open the door and ushered her in.

Emily narrowed her eyes against the gloom. She could make out a table by the window and a sofa in front of the fireplace. The interior was rustic at best. She hugged herself as a wave of disquiet swamped her. She was alone with a man. In a cramped cabin. On an isolated island.

She'd been alone with a man in an isolated spot once before.

That had been a catastrophe.

"I'll start a fire. Can you light those lamps?"

The sound of his deep voiced snapped her from a dark memory and she started. "Lamps?"

"I see two on the mantel."

Ah. Yes. She swallowed heavily and crossed the room. There were, indeed, two kerosene lamps on the mantel, and a box of matches. She carried them to the table, where there was a hint of sunshine, and worked on trying to figure out how to light them while he set a fire.

When the first one flared, chasing away the shadows, she felt better. The second illuminated the room even more.

It was actually quite charming, she decided. Homey. There was a door on the other side of the cabin, which she assumed was a bathroom and another next to it, which was probably a closet. Even as her stomach growled, her gaze stalled on a cupboard by the fireplace. She carried one of the lamps over, opened the door and found it stocked with staples.

She shot a glance over her shoulder to find Ash watching her. A fire crackled cheerily behind his kneeling form, surrounding him with a warm circle of light. For some reason, the sight of that halo calmed her nerves.

"We won't starve," she said.

"I'm glad to hear it. What's in there?" He stood and brushed off his knees and came over to check out the fare.

"Let's see. A can of peaches, pancake mix, condensed milk, coffee." She shot him a grin. "Spam."

"Spam?"

"Spam, spam, spam, spam," she sang, delighted when he laughed.

"Ooh, caviar." He pulled out a fancy jar.

She wrinkled her nose.

"What? You don't like caviar?"

"Ick. I'd rather eat a bug."

"Really?" He scanned the contents of the cupboard. "Any bugs in there?"

She snorted a chuckle. She couldn't help it.

"Oh, there's wine." He pulled out a bottle of merlot. "Do you like red?"

Again, she wrinkled her nose. "I'm not much of a drinker."

"One glass?"

She shrugged. "Maybe one glass."

He hunted for a minute, coming up with a bottle opener and two tin cups. He held them up with a wink. "Classy."

"With a 'K.'" She plucked at her damp pant legs. The clinging fabric annoyed her.

"Do you want to take those off?" he asked.

Her pulse lurched. "Wh-what?"

"You can dry them by the fire."

"Oh, no. That's okay," she said. She wore a long shirt beneath her overalls, but the thought of prancing before him with bare legs set her teeth on edge. She would rather be a little uncomfortable.

She pulled out a box of crackers and arranged them on a plate, spreading them with peanut butter from a jar in the back, and then arranged their feast on the table. They sat, limned in the glow of the fire and the flickering lamps, and dined. On peanut butter and crackers and merlot. An odd combination, but she enjoyed it. Because he was there.

While they ate, they chatted about his glasswork and her glasswork and pets they'd had and nothing much in particular. The merlot was delicious. She had two tin cups full—more, perhaps, because he kept topping hers off. It lit a spark within her, singing in her veins. By the time they finished eating, she was feeling particularly mellow.

As she tidied up, putting the peanut butter and crackers back in the cupboard—the wine she left out because he said he wanted more later—he explored the cabin, opening the two doors and peering inside.

The first door did indeed lead to a bathroom, which Emily found comforting. She didn't relish the idea of relieving herself in the woods.

He opened the second door and grunted, "There are sheets in the closet. I wonder if the sofa is a fold out." He crossed the room and pulled off the cushions, revealing a hide-a-bed, which he pulled up and out. Expanded, the bed took up most of the small space. "You can sleep here," he said. "I'll sleep on the floor."

Emily winced. The floor was hardwood. It would probably be very uncomfortable. "That's not fair," she said. "I'll sleep on the floor."

Ash put his fists on his hips and mock-glared at her. "There's no way you're sleeping on the floor. A gentleman always lets the lady take the bed."

She nearly sighed. He was so chivalrous. In her experience, men that handsome were…less than chivalrous.

She opened her mouth and the words slipped out. "We can share the bed."

Egads. Had she actually said that? Her heart thudded, awaiting his response. To her relief, his reaction was nothing more than a friendly nod.

"Okay." He turned away, back to the closet, riffling through it. He pulled out sheets and pillows and blankets, which he piled on the back of the sofa. "Are you a lefty or a righty?"

"A what?" She laughed and picked up the bottom sheet, ignoring her shaking hands. He took hold of one corner and together they fanned it out over the mattress. She couldn't meet his gaze. This was all far too intimate.

But he was so matter-of-fact. That, in itself, calmed her.

"Do you sleep on the right or the left when you share a bed?"

Emily swallowed the lump in her throat. She didn't know. She'd never shared a bed. Never *slept* with a man. "I…ah… It doesn't matter."

"I usually sleep on the left."

"O-okay."

He whipped out the blanket. She watched it billow, trying to calm the sudden churning in her belly. He tossed two pillows onto the head of the bed.

Two. Pillows.

It hit home then.

He would be sleeping there. Next to her.

Her pulse surged. "Sh-should w-we put something b-between us?"

"Like a sword?" His expression could have been scorching, but it was difficult to tell because it was hooded. He smiled. A casual smile, but she noticed the tense lines around his mouth. He was probably as nervous as she about all this.

"Th-that's what they did in the olden days." The chivalrous knights.

"I don't, ahem, have a sword." And then he murmured something that sounded like, *"Not that kind of sword,"* but she couldn't be sure.

She scouted the room for something. Something that would create a barrier, make her feel safe. Which was stupid. He was a decent guy. He'd kissed her once, and it had been a wonderful kiss, but he hadn't pounced upon her or grabbed her or backed her into a corner. He hadn't said or done anything even remotely sleazy. Still, when her gaze landed on the broomstick in the closet, she let out a gusty sigh. "This." She grabbed the broom, arranged it on the bed, right in the middle and then glanced at him.

His lips quirked, as though her whimsy amused him. He nodded. "Perfect." He yawned. "Are you ready for bed?"

"No." She didn't mean the word to come out that sharply, but the prospect of crawling into bed with him, broomstick or not, petrified her.

"Okay. How about a game of cards, then?" He pulled a deck from a drawer in the end table and shuffled.

"What would you like to play?"

He shrugged. "Poker?"

She wandered to the table by the window and sat. "I don't know how to play poker."

"Perfect."

She grinned at his expression. "How about gin rummy?" His face fell, but it was such an overblown pout, she knew he was teasing her.

"Oh, all right." He dealt the cards, then poured them each another tin cup of wine.

They played for a while, chatting and sipping their wine. It was a pleasant evening. He was a charming companion, asking her about her life as a teacher and chattering on about television shows and movies they both liked. They had several favorite restaurants in common and even had a few mutual friends.

He reached for the bottle and refilled her glass, but when he went to refill his own, the bottle was empty. "Shall I open another?" he asked.

Emily nibbled her lip. She loved this cozy, contented feeling. She knew it came from the rich, buttery merlot, but she didn't think she should have any more. However, she didn't want this to end. Not yet. "Sure."

He practically sprinted across the room to the pantry, coming back with another bottle. They continued to play and drink and talk until the fire died down. He tossed on another log and stretched.

"Well," he said. "We should probably turn in."

"Mmm hmm." She fought back a yawn. When she stood, she teetered and grabbed the back of the chair for balance. "Oh my. I think I drank a bit too much." Her chuckle stalled in her throat as she caught his look. It seemed almost…predatory. Then he blinked and that friendly countenance was back in place. She must have imagined it. "I…ah…think I need to use the facilities."

Other than a grunt, he didn't respond. He occupied himself smoothing the blanket on the bed and fluffing the pillows.

When she emerged from the bathroom, and saw him already in bed, under the covers, dismay claimed her. Heavens. How was she going to do this? How was she going to fall asleep next to him? Her instinct for survival would not allow it.

But there was more to it than that with Ash. With Ash she felt a draw, an urge she'd never felt before.

It tasted like…temptation.

With Ash, she wanted the intimacy she'd eschewed for the entirety of her adult life. Sure, it still scared her, the thought of being with a man like that, but she wanted it.

She craved it.

That scared her too.

She contemplated grabbing a pillow and a blanket and curling up on the floor, despite their broomstick negotiations, but decided not to. She wouldn't want him to think she was some kind of weird woman. Besides, he was very definitely on his side of the bed. His shoulder rose and fell in an even pattern. Perhaps he was already asleep?

Why her mood dipped at the prospect was a mystery.

When she perched on her side of the bed, he rolled over.

"Are you going to take your overalls off?"

She glanced at him. "I-I wasn't going to." The fabric was still damp at the cuffs, but the thought of sloughing off her armor was terrifying.

"Might be uncomfortable, sleeping in them." He winked. "I promise not to look." He covered his eyes.

She giggled, because he was being silly, and unhooked one strap and then the other. If she'd been wearing a bathing suit, he'd see more, she told herself. "Are your eyes closed?"

"Mmm hmm."

She stood, shimmied the overalls off and draped them on a chair by the fire. When she turned around, his eyes weren't closed, or covered. He was watching her.

"You promised not to look."

He grinned. "Have I mentioned I'm a liar?"

Why this confession made her laugh, she didn't know. Probably because she didn't believe him. He was so cute. So funny. And, she had to admit it, she was tipsy. Okay, maybe more than tipsy.

She lifted the covers and slipped into the bed, being very careful to perch on the very edge. Holding herself as rigid as she could, she laced her fingers over her tummy and studied the ceiling. The flickering light of the fire illuminated the room in a soft glow. It wasn't hot. It certainly didn't account for the warmth rising on her cheeks.

No, that was due to his intent gaze. He propped up on his elbow and stared at her.

Like a frightened doe, she flicked a quick peep at him, and then looked away.

"Emily." His voice was dark, deep.

"Yes, Ash?" This, she chirped.

"You are so beautiful."

"Thank you." She winced. Damn it. She'd spent her whole life living within a strict code of behavior. Politeness, so deeply engrained in her, did not allow her to stray.

"I…ah… May I kiss you goodnight?"

Her pulse fluttered. Her attention snapped to his face. His lips were alluring, full. She'd loved that first kiss he'd given her. Barely been able to stop thinking about it.

One part of her brain cautioned she should say no. They were alone. In a remote cabin. In bed. Surely allowing a kiss, in these circumstances, would be tantamount to an invitation for more.

But this was Ash.

The most handsome, charming, sweet fellow she'd ever met. She felt a connection with him. A connection unlike any she'd ever felt with a man.

She steeled her spine and levered up. She intended it to be a quick peck, but when their lips touched, when she tasted his breath and felt the damp heat of his mouth, she couldn't pull away.

CHAPTER FIVE

Yes. Yes. Yes. She was kissing him.

Lust snarled in Ash's gut. It had been snarling there all fucking night, but now it rose to a howl. It had been torture, sitting there, chatting with her, putting her at ease, when all he'd wanted to do was pounce. Pull her into his arms, entice her into his bed, and make crazy passionate love to her.

But he'd known. He'd sensed her reserve. So he'd gone slow.

Okay, the wine had been a douche move, but he'd given her plenty of opportunities to say no. And she hadn't. And now she was kissing him.

Ash changed the tenor of the kiss, slowly nudging it into something far sultrier. Seductive.

She murmured, moaned. Her fingers skated along his nape and into his hair. He shuddered as she lightly raked his scalp.

Damn, she was sexy. Everything about her was sexy. When she'd slipped out of those overalls, revealing a flowing shirt that fell nearly to her knees, his cock had twanged painfully. Even dressed like that, she was irresistible.

"Emily," he edged closer, pulling her against him. Something prodded his belly. The ridiculous broomstick. He fumbled for it, wrenched it away, tossed it to the floor.

Her lips moved—perhaps in protest?—so he dabbed his tongue into her mouth. She whimpered a little. Held him tighter. He turned her head and made his way over her cheek to nibble on her neck. She sighed. He stroked her breast, thumbed a nipple. It was hard. A thick, swollen bud. Even through her bra. She cried out and pushed into him, curling a leg over his hip, sealing them at the groin. His cock jerked.

Yeah, she was reserved. Yeah, she had a cloak of propriety wrapped firmly around her. But beneath the surface lay a deeply passionate woman.

He fumbled with the blanket until he found the soft smooth skin of her bare thigh. He shuddered as he edged up and up. Cupped her ass. Damn, she had a fine ass. Curvy and firm. Supple. He'd suspected it, but it had been impossible to tell through her thick overalls.

He slid beneath the elastic band of her panties, over that sweet flesh, and squeezed.

She made a tiny sound and wriggled.

He nearly lost consciousness. She felt so good in his arms. So fucking right. And she smelled like heaven. The heady combination of jasmine and arousal made his head swim. "Emily," he moaned. "Emily."

Swallowing heavily, he unbuttoned her blouse with his free hand. It took a while because the buttons were so damn small and it was a weird angle. But he persevered, rewarded with a glimpse of a lacy bra and the deep shadow of her cleavage. His fingers on her ass involuntarily tightened. Shit. Shit. She was amazing.

"God." He yanked out of her panties, though it nearly killed him to do so, and laid her back, cupping her breasts with both hands. Her bra had a front hook, thank God, which he deftly worked. And those glorious globes spilled out.

"Ash…" He disliked the hint of reproach in her tone, so he ignored it and took one pink crest into his mouth, and sucked. She cried out, a warble of delight, so he did the same with the other. He went back and forth, exploring, tasting. "Ash…"

No reproach now. The word sounded more like a plea.

He eased a palm down her abdomen and over her stomach, coming to a halt over her warm mound. Every one of his muscles clenched. She froze as well.

He raised his head, captured her gaze, and slowly traced her cleft. She gasped. Tiny tears dewed her lashes. "Ash," she breathed. And she arched up. Just a tiny lift of her hips, and in doing so, her nether lips parted. Through the lace of her panties, he traced her clit.

Her body quivered. She groaned, then cried out.

He'd been with a lot of women. He knew the signs. If he wasn't mistaken, she'd just come. He stroked her again. And again, through the rough material, circling her nub, reveling in the cream soaking through, soaking her. Soaking him.

God, his cock ached. He wanted her, wanted in, with every fiber of his being. Madly, he fumbled for the condom he'd set on the end table. He ripped it open and slipped it on, all the while rubbing her slit and sucking her nipples. She writhed beneath him, which made him mad with lust.

When he was ready, he pulled the blankets off and pulled down her panties. He shuddered when he stroked her clit again, skin to skin. She was soaked. Fucking soaked.

Trembling, he levered over her, spread her knees with his and set his cock to the mouth of her cunt. Her heat scalded him. Maddened him. "Emily," he groaned, and pushed in.

His heart seized. Goddamn, she was tight. Almost too tight.

"Ash?" she murmured, cupping his cheek. "Ash?"

He stilled, ensnared by her expression. "Yes?" A whisper.

"Be gentle." As she spoke the words, the folds of her cunt, clinging to the tip of his cock, undulated, sipped at him and he nearly lost his mind. "Oh yeah," he growled. "Gentle." And he thrust.

There was a little resistance at first, a rigid ring of muscles at her entrance that inflamed him, but once he was past it, he filled her with an effortless lunge. She jerked; the undulations of her folds sent prickles of pleasure dancing up his spine.

Holy fuck. He closed his eyes against the bliss of her slick, taut embrace. He'd been hungry for this, aching for this for hours.

He pulled out and thrust in again. And again. Colors danced on the inside of his lids. Shivers shimmied through him. Agony seethed in his balls. He gritted his teeth in an effort to hold back. It was too good, too damn good to be over so quickly.

She grunted and lifted her knees, cradling him. "Yeah, oh yeah," he rumbled and sank deeper. He pressed her breasts together, burying his face between them and drawing in her scent.

"Ash…"

He thumbed her nipples, gave them a tweak and, liking her response, did it again. He played with her, toyed with her as he worked in and out of her excruciatingly firm grasp.

He glanced at her. The tears he'd noticed earlier now tracked into her hair. Her lips parted. Her pupils dilated. God, she was gorgeous like this. Beneath him, gazing up at him. While he was buried in her depths.

His cock surged. The burn of cum boiling to erupt seared him.

But he wanted her to come too. Come with him.

He reached down between them and thumbed her clit. She cried out, clutched at him, scored his shoulders with her nails.

"Yes." He liked that. She did it again as he sank deep one last time. "Yes. Yes. Yes."

And he erupted.

Scalding insanity flooded his heart, his mind, his soul, as he emptied into her in wave after rushing wave. A surge of peace, of bliss, of serenity filled him. He nestled against her neck and huffed out a laugh.

God. She'd been magnificent.

* * * * *

Emily lay motionless, though Ash's weight on her was becoming uncomfortable. She stared up at the ceiling as she waited for his breathing to return to normal.

So that was it, she thought. That was all it was?

She shouldn't have this sense of disappointment. Really, she shouldn't. She'd probably built it up in her mind as this great transcendent sharing, some spiritual melding that left both parties irrevocably changed.

Oh, it had been nice. It had been pleasant. And there had been that bit of bliss when he'd toyed with her…down there. But then he'd climbed on top and pushed his way inside her and he'd been huge and, well, it had hurt a bit.

Maybe she'd done something wrong.

But he'd seemed to enjoy it. A lot. Huffing and grunting and howling her name.

She shouldn't be disappointed.

If nothing else, she'd finally *done it*.

It had to happen sometime and wouldn't she want it to be with a man like him?

She feathered her fingers through his hair and held him close. If it was going to be anyone, she was glad it was Ash.

Because she liked him. She liked him a lot.

His kiss, his laugh, his sense of humor. The glowing aura that always seemed to surround him. Everything. She liked everything about him.

And now that she'd finally done it, on her own terms, there was nothing to be afraid of. Not anymore.

He kissed her, a brief buss, and rolled off. She gusted out a breath. He settled beside her, punching his pillow under his head so he could gaze at her. "That was great," he said.

She smiled shyly and pulled the covers back up. "Thank you," she said, hoping for another kiss.

But he didn't kiss her. He rolled over, showing her his back, and punched his pillow again before settling down. Within moments, a low snore rumbled through the room.

She glared at him—only because he couldn't see.

Seriously?

She knew she'd read far too many fairy tales as a child and far too many romances as a young girl. She knew her expectations were unrealistic and fanciful and, all right, a bit naïve.

But she had never, in the whole of her life, imagined her Prince Charming would snore.

* * * * *

Emily woke up in the morning feeling achy and stiff. She glanced over at Ash, to see he was still asleep. She slipped from the bed and visited the bathroom, relieved to find several wrapped toothbrushes in the cabinet.

When she was finished with her ablutions, she padded back out into the main room and found her panties in the tangle of sheets. Though she blushed at the memory of what they'd done last night, she didn't bother with her bra.

He continued to snooze even though she made a bit of noise fixing coffee in an old metal percolator, which she set on a rack over the fire she'd built. She whipped up a batch of pancakes, cooking them on the same makeshift grill over the fire in a heavy iron skillet. It was kind of fun. Like camping, only indoors, and without all the mosquitoes.

By the time the pancakes were ready, he'd roused.

"Morning," he mumbled, propping himself against the back of the sofa bed.

"Good morning," she said, flipping a pancake on to a plate. "Are you hungry?"

"Famished."

She was thankful that he tugged on his briefs before he padded to the table. Oh, certainly they'd been wound together in the bed last night, and he'd been nearly naked then, but breakfast was another thing entirely. She didn't think she could sit here and eat next to a man who didn't have any underwear on. Propriety would be offended.

He took a sip of his coffee and groaned. "Excellent," he said. "But these pancakes need syrup."

She shrugged and cut into hers, popping a bite into her mouth. "I didn't see any."

He grunted and stood, heading across the room to the pantry. He bent and opened one of the lower cupboards, one she hadn't noticed, over to the side, and pulled out a bottle of syrup. Her fork froze, halfway to her mouth. How had he known that was there?

"Have you...have you been here before?"

He stilled. "Ah... Once or twice. Do you want more coffee?"

"Please." He brought the pot and topped off both their cups, though his was nearly full. He set the pot on the table, plopped back in his chair and wolfed down his pancakes.

"These are really good," he said.

"There's more." When he glanced up at her, she smiled. "I made extra. I figured you'd be hungry."

"Oh, I'm hungry." His expression made it clear he wasn't talking about pancakes. "You look cute in that big shirt."

She blushed. "Someone popped off a button," she said, thumbing the gaping spot. She'd buttoned it all the way up. Though they'd made love last night, she wasn't comfortable enough around him to wander about flashing her private bits.

"Someone should have ripped off more." His foot nudged hers under the table. She thought it was an accident, but then it made its way up her calf. Over her knee. Up her thigh.

"Ash," she laughed, scooting back. "It's breakfast."

"Perfect time for it." He waggled his brows.

"I think not," she said primly, though she loved his playful mood. She cut a precise slice out of her pancake, doused it with syrup and popped it into her mouth. Then she licked the fork clean.

He snorted. "Do you know what that makes me want to do?"

The light in his eyes stunned her. "W-what?"

"Come here." Even as he said the words, he reached around the table and grabbed the base of her chair, scooting her over next to him. The wood legs screeched across the floor. He pulled her onto his lap and she shifted to get comfortable. A firm bulge surged against her hip.

He yanked open her blouse, sending buttons skittering across the table. "Ash!"

"Hush." He picked up the bottle of syrup and drizzled it over her chest.

She gasped. "Ash, you're getting it all over me."

He grinned. "That would be the point." His tongue was like slick velvet as he licked the sticky substance from her breasts. And then he decorated her with more. And feasted on her again. His touch made shivers ripple over her skin. Made her shudder. Made her quake.

"Humph." He grunted around the nipple in his mouth.

"What?"

He didn't respond. He merely lifted her in his arms, despite her squeal, and carried her to the bed. She bounced as he tossed her on the mattress. "Hold still."

She did not. She leaned up on her elbows and watched as he padded back to the table and grabbed the bottle. "Oh no! Oh no!"

"Oh yes."

She tried to wriggle away, but was laughing too hard. He leaped onto the bed, held her down and kissed her. He tasted sweet and sinful. "Hold still."

He arranged her on the bed, and she held as still as she could…but for the quivering. When he set her arms over her head and spread the lapels of her shirt, she allowed it, but when he nudged her knees apart, she resisted. He shot her a wicked, seductive glance. "Come on, Emily. I want some more breakfast."

"I am not breakfast—" Her protest ended in a squeal as he dripped a healthy serving of syrup…all over her panties. "Ash!"

"Mmm. I love syrup." He swooped in and lapped.

Every muscle clenched. "Ash."

He lifted his head and stared at her. His jocularity melted away. Something dark and hungry flickered over his features. He lowered his head again. This time, his foray was far more deliberate. Far more intense.

He found and dabbed her sensitive center. As he teased her through the lace, heat rose in her womb. He worked her, cleaned her with diligent attention, and before long she was nearly mindless with need. She wiggled her hips. "Please," she moaned. "Please."

The look in his eye made her shudder. He drew her panties down, opened her with his thumbs and went back to work.

She nearly came out of her skin as he traced her slit, then delved deeper, nudging the folds of her labia. When he suckled her, delicious sensation shot through to her core, sending ripples of exquisite pleasure shimmering out in waves.

"Yes," she sighed. "Yes." This was it. This was the bliss she'd felt last night…and more.

He slid a finger in and she winced. She hadn't liked that much last night. Not at all.

But this… Oh. But this! Nuzzling her swollen clit, he eased in another and explored her depths. She wailed, groaned, flailed as he found a spot, over to the side that sent a dull thrum rippling through her. *More*, she thought. *More. More. More.*

He gave her more, moving around in a hypnotizing rhythm, filling her, withdrawing, and then filling her again. Tapping that spot, scraping it, making her wild with need.

"Ash," she panted. "Ash. Please."

He came over her, kissing his way up, a quick, impatient journey.

She cupped his cock, annoyed at the cotton she found. He yanked his underwear down and she fisted him. Ah. He was hard and warm and smooth. She pumped his length. He gave a growl, so she did it again.

"Emily." He adjusted his hips and nudged her center. Taking her nipple between his lips, he sucked as he pressed in.

She nearly swooned.

This was different. This was…better. So much better.

"Yes," she cried as he lunged in, sinking deep.

He sucked in a breath as she closed around him. She tightened her muscles, testing his girth. His nostrils flared. "Shit," he muttered. She clenched harder and he groaned. Buried his face in her hair. "Jesus."

He yanked out—she nearly howled—but then he thrust deep again and God, it was glorious. He nudged her knees further apart and began a series of long slow slides. Each one sent her higher and higher, into some ethereal realm. She curled around him, her arms, her legs, her everything. Curled around him and clung as he worked away inside her.

Just when she thought she might scream, when she could no longer bear this agonizingly deliberate pace, his tempo increased, grew in intensity. He found that spot again and aimed for it, pounding into it with each manic thrust. And with each stroke, she lost a little of herself, spinning faster and faster, higher and higher, like a whirling dervish.

And then she spun free, sailed into space and floated, suspended in a welter of mindless rapture as absolute bliss consumed her.

She'd never known. Never imagined. Never dreamed…

He swelled inside her. Filled her even more, massaged her even more completely and, unbelievably, she shot even higher. The dam broke. Her core liquefied. A warm wet heat flooded her.

He continued moving, after the ecstasy had peaked, drawing it out, sending tingles upon tingles through her quivering body. And then he slowed. Stopped.

When she opened her eyes, he was staring down at her with the most gentle, loving look. She smiled. He smiled back. And he kissed her. And she knew.

Yes. This was the fairy tale. This was the dream come true.

He was her Prince Charming after all.

CHAPTER SIX

This time, when they tried to start the Jet Ski, it worked. They'd cleaned up after their passionate tryst, putting away the sheets and folding up the bed, tidying up the pots and pans and putting everything back where they'd found it. And then they'd dressed and headed back to the beach.

It was early morning; the marine layer curled over the water in a delicate mist. But it was time to go back, he said, and Emily couldn't protest. Her friends would be worried about her, if they'd realized she was missing. She had dropped her stuff in the small bedroom in the garret, so the others might have assumed she'd gone to bed early. They might not even have noticed she hadn't come home.

She hoped they hadn't noticed. If she could sneak back into the house and slip into bed, it would avoid so much explaining.

Ash powered the craft back to his beach and moored it. When he cut the engine, the silence was deafening. He handed her up on to the dock and then followed. They stood there, staring at each other. She hated the awkwardness of the moment, but it was probably a moment many women had experienced.

After.

"Well," she said.

"Well." His gaze flickered.

"I suppose I should get back?" She hadn't intended it as a question, but really, it was.

"Probably a good idea." Why her mood plummeted when he agreed was a mystery. Or not. They walked to the end of the dock and stepped onto the beach.

"I…ah… Thank you for the ride." She tried not to wince at the idiocy of her statement but she couldn't think of anything else to say.

His lips quirked. "Thank you…for the ride." She didn't understand his words at first, but then his meaning percolated through her brain and she colored.

"Ahem. Well. I'll see you around this weekend?" Another question that shouldn't have been one at all.

"Yeah," he said. "See you around."

And then, to her dismay, he shoved his hands in his pockets, spun on his heel and headed up the path to his place.

Okay. She hadn't expected a declaration of undying love. But a kiss would have been nice. Or a hug. Or a smile. Something.

She hated that she watched until he disappeared from view. She should have turned away, just as he had, and gone straight home instead of mooning after him like some lovelorn calf.

She grimaced when she realized she'd left her hat at the cabin.

Damn it all. It was her favorite hat.

Surely that was why tears pricked at her lashes.

That and nothing else.

"Where the hell have you been?" Bella bellowed as Emily opened the back door.

So much for slipping in unnoticed. They were all there in the kitchen, Holt and Bella and Kaitlin and Jamie and Tara. It was like the cast of *Ben Hur* in that kitchen. "I went to your room this morning and your bed hadn't been slept in."

"I told you she was safe," Kaitlin murmured.

"Damn it Emily," Bella's voice rose into a wail. "We've been worried sick."

Emily winced. She disliked yelling. Did not allow it in her classroom. And Bella could really yell. "I'm sorry. Ash took me out for a ride on his Jet Ski last night—"

"Last night?" Tara parroted.

Bella's nose curled. "Ash?"

"And the motor conked out."

Holt bristled. "The motor conked out?"

"We-we had to spend the night on the island." A blush crept up her cheeks.

"You had to spend the night on the island?" This, Holt ground through his teeth.

"It was getting dark. And it's too far to swim back. And the tide was going out..." Ooh. She didn't like the feral glint in his eyes. His muscles bunched, even when Bella set a hand on his arm. "There's a cabin there," she finished lamely.

"I will fucking kill him."

"Holt!" Heavens. He was furious.

Drew Boone padded barefoot into the kitchen in a pair of baggy sweats. Apparently he'd arrived during the night. "Kill who?"

"Ash Fucking Bristol."

Drew blinked. His gaze danced from Holt to Emily and back again. "Oookay."

"He took Emily for a ride. To the *island*." Holt said it like it was secret code or something, but Drew caught his meaning immediately.

Great. Now they were both glaring at her.

Drew raked his hair until it stood on end. "Why the hell would you let Ash Bristol take you for a ride...anywhere?"

Emily folded her hands. "He seemed nice."

"Nice?" Drew's roar rocked the room. "He's a fucking barracuda. He eats little girls like you for breakfast."

Now her cheeks were scalding. He had. Eaten her for breakfast. And she'd loved it.

"There's only one reason a guy takes a woman to that island. One reason." Holt shoved his finger in her face.

The teacher inside her rose to the fore. Gently, politely, she shoved it out of the way. It was either that or bite it off.

"Seduction," Drew growled.

Emily frowned. "We just went for a ride. It's hardly his fault the engine conked out."

"He told her the engine conked out?" Drew asked Holt, although clearly he did not expect a response. "That's the oldest trick in the fucking book."

"Please watch your language."

"He's not cursing," Holt snapped. "It's the Fucking Book. The Fucking Playbook."

"Seduction 101."

"I'm not listening to this." Emily pushed past them both and into the living room. It took some effort because they were both so big and so annoyed and not inclined to make room for her.

"Did he fuck you?" Drew asked, although it was absolutely none of his business. Emily didn't respond, so he asked again, in a louder voice. Which, according to the Neanderthal Playbook, usually worked.

But Emily was not a Neanderthal woman. She was a modern woman in charge of her own body. She made her own decisions and she dealt with the consequences appropriately. She sailed through the room, not making eye contact with any of the women, and then she pounded up the stairs to her room, ignoring Drew's heated stare.

"Because if he fucked you," he shouted, "I'm gonna fucking kill him."

She didn't respond, other than to slam her door. And then she opened it. And slammed it again for good measure.

* * * * *

Okay, he shouldn't have just walked away.

He knew better.

He should have told her then. Just steeled his spine and opened his mouth and said, "Thanks for the memories, babe. It was fun." But somehow he couldn't. Ash had the weird suspicion those words would hurt her, destroy her maybe.

But she was a grown up. She knew the score. A clean break was the best way. He was sure of it. One night only. That was the rule.

So he ignored the niggle of guilt and walked away.

Once he got onto his deck though, shadowed by the trees, he turned. And he watched as she plodded back to the house next door.

He quit watching when the guilt got too sharp. With a self-directed snort, he wrenched the sliding glass door open and winced. *Shit.* What was that smell?

It didn't take him long to figure it out. Because he stepped in it. A thick, slimy pile of vomit on the hardwood floor. And on the Turkish carpet. And on the leather sofa.

Clearly one of his friends, who'd had way too much to drink, had been sick in the night. Probably Richie.

Probably Richie, because he'd been so shitfaced. And because, there he was, lying in an odd tangle on the un-christened sofa, covered in flop sweat and snoring up a storm.

For the umpteenth time, Ash asked himself why he even invited Richie to come over. He almost always fucked something up. He thought about leaving the mess, but then he realized, Richie didn't clean up after himself, and by the time the ass regained consciousness, the stains would only be worse. The maid didn't come until Monday.

So he grabbed a bucket of soapy water, some rubber gloves and a couple rolls of paper towels and dove into the unpleasant task. He tried not to think about *her* while he worked, but he couldn't help reliving every second they'd spent together. He'd enjoyed their conversations the most, the way her eyes lit up, the way she laughed when she talked about her dogs or her students. Some of her stories had been hysterical.

But he'd loved kissing her, making love to her, more. Especially this morning. She'd been so responsive, fit him like a glove.

It was a damn shame he couldn't just go over there and ask her to go for another ride on his Jet Ski. She'd probably say yes. But that would be leading her on.

He wasn't the kind of guy who could have a lasting relationship with a woman. He didn't come from those kinds of people. He didn't have that kind of luck. He'd never found the right kind of girl.

Which sucked.

What he really wanted was to relax into a relationship. Trust in her. But every time he let a flirtation, an affair, drift into a relationship, he got stung. Always.

There were no happily ever afters for a guy like him. He'd have to settle for happy endings.

Hence the One Night Stand Rule.

One time. That was it.

Fuck 'em and walk away.

No matter what.

And it worked. His heart hadn't been broken once since he'd put the practice into play. He ignored the hollow satisfaction at the thought. Ignored the image of Emily's expression as she'd come around him. The sweet lines of her face as he watched her while she slept.

He'd loved sleeping with her. Loved waking up with her.

Loved pretending, for one night, it could be something other than what it was.

But it was morning now. And he knew better.

Sure, Emily seemed like a sweet girl. They all did at first. Before they got their hooks in a guy. And she was a teacher. *A teacher*. Ash knew, deep down, she was just like all the others. Sooner or later, she'd try something, like Teresa, who'd come to him, after a short fling, announcing she was pregnant with his child.

Oh, she'd been pregnant. Just not with the Bristol heir. Some other peckerwood had planted his seed in her and she'd seen a big payday coming.

Thank God for DNA testing.

And a rabid legal team.

Ash had been super careful after that. Always carrying a condom with him. Never forgetting to use protection—

His scrubbing slowed as a memory flashed in his brain. Slipping into Emily. How slick she'd been. How wet. How intense.

Fuck it all to hell. No wonder it had been so fucking incredible.

Goddamn it.

He had.

This morning he'd been so crazed by her scent, her moans and the rake of her nails over his scalp as he ate her out, he'd completely forgotten to use a condom.

He threw the sponge into the bucket. It sloshed over the carpet. How could he have been so stupid? It was her fault. She had to be so damn pretty, with that soft, low voice, those wide tempting eyes. She had to drive a man crazy with lust until he covered her and shoved it in without a thought to the consequences.

Dumb.

Dumb, dumb, dumb.

If nothing else convinced him she was, in fact, one dangerous woman, that should.

He'd made the right decision.

Yeah. He had to steer clear of Emily—

His breath caught as he searched for her last name.

Well fuck. He didn't know it.

Fine.

That was just fine.

He didn't want to know it.

He didn't.

"God, it stinks in here," Parker muttered through a sleep-roughened voice as he padded down the stairs. "What the hell happened?"

Ash sighed and gestured toward Richie, who snuffled and grunted and blubbered in his sleep.

"Jesus." Parker grimaced and headed for the kitchen, finding another pair of gloves under the sink. He pitched in, which was awesome, because Ash was getting nauseous. Together, they finished the job pretty quickly, tossed the paper towels and the sponges into a trash bag and put it out on the back deck. "He was pretty loaded last night."

"He's pretty loaded every night." Ash led the way back to the kitchen and they washed their hands in the sink. Several times. Then he pushed the button to start the coffee pot. The grinder kicked into gear with a loud wail. On the sofa, Richie lurched up and gazed around the room with bleary eyes.

"Where did you disappear to last night?" Parker asked, getting two matching mugs from the cupboard.

Ash shot him a look. "Nowhere."

"He went out on the Jet Ski," Richie said, shuffling into the kitchen, scratching his pits and yawning. He wore a t-shirt and shorts speckled with not-so-mysterious stains. The clothes clung to his body, damp with sweat. "I heard it start up when I was taking a piss." He waggled a finger at Ash. "Did you find a chickie?"

"Go take a shower, Richie. You reek."

Richie's nose curled. "This whole place reeks." Ash and Parker exchanged a glance. "Was it that hot redhead? Or the honey with the ponytail? The one with the bangs was cute too."

"Shut up Richie." Ash's pulse throbbed painfully in his temple.

"Which one did you bang?"

Acid curled in his gut. "Shut up, Richie." Richie was a bonafide asshole sometimes.

Parker stepped between them, which was hardly necessary. It wasn't as though Ash was going to pound Richie's nose in. Much. "Come on, Richie.

41

You know Ash doesn't kiss and tell."

Richie glowered at him, and then the tension dissolved as he barked a laugh. "No. He never does. Doesn't fuck and tell, either. Which sucks. Because it would help to know."

"Know what?" A growl.

"Which one is easy."

Easy? *Easy?*

Easy was reaching around Parker and slamming his fist into Richie's smug face.

It was also gratifying.

CHAPTER SEVEN

Emily had stripped off her clothes, dropping them onto a pile on the floor, and changed into her bathing suit and cover up when the soft knock came at the door. She kicked her overalls aside and padded across the room. She'd never wear that outfit again. The blouse was missing all of its buttons for one thing, and for another, everything smelled like him.

She opened the door and peered through the crack at Kaitlin. Her heart wobbled. Somehow Kaitlin always knew when Emily needed a friend.

"Are you okay?" she asked in a soft voice.

"Is she?" Bella popped her head around Kaitlin's shoulder. *Great.* Bella was there as well. "Is she all right?"

"Is she?"

Really? Jamie too?

"Is everyone up here?" Emily asked on a sigh.

"No."

"Thank God."

"Cam and Kristi are asleep, and Tara is distracting Drew and Holt." Bella grinned.

Emily frowned. "Drew and Holt are not coming up here." That was the last thing she needed right now.

"They're making bacon," Kaitlin said in a soothing voice. As though she sensed Emily's flaring panic. "Can we come in?"

"They're making bacon?"

"For you." Jamie pushed around Kaitlin and into the room.

Emily stepped back and let them all in. As though she had a choice. "Why are they making bacon for me?"

"Drew feels bad about yelling," Kaitlin said.

At the same time, Bella quipped, "Because they want to lure you back downstairs and get the details of…" she trailed off and glanced around at all the glares. "What? It's true."

"Shut up Bella," Jamie snapped. "We're supposed to be calming her down."

Kaitlin shot Emily an apologetic look. "I should have come alone."

"I'm fine. Honestly. You can all go back downstairs and—"

Bella sidled up to Emily and sniffed her. *Sniffed her.* "Why do you smell like maple syrup?"

"I-I d-don't."

"You do." Bella waved at the others. "Come over here. Smell her."

Kaitlin crossed her arms. "I'm not smelling anyone. Leave her alone Bella."

"I'm telling you. She smells like syrup."

"Stop it. You're making her cry." Jamie wrapped an arm around Emily's shoulder and, to her horror, she realized she was, indeed, leaking tears.

"I-I'm not crying."

"What's that on your cheeks? Aunt Jemima?"

"Bella." A warning growl from Kaitlin. This caught Bella's attention, because Kaitlin hardly ever growled. "I think you should both go," she said. "Emily and I need to have a talk."

Bella put out a lip.

"*I* didn't make her cry," Jamie protested.

But Kaitlin was adamant. She thrust a slender finger at the door. "Go."

"All right," Bella huffed. "We'll be just outside in the hall if you need us."

"I'm sorry about that," Kaitlin said, closing the door. She crossed to the bed and sat, patting the spot beside her. "I told them I needed to come alone but they wouldn't listen."

"Because they wanted to grill me."

Kaitlin's bow-shaped mouth tweaked up. "A little. But they also care about you. A lot." She cocked her head to the side in that funny way she had and studied Emily, her eyes slightly unfocused. "Something happened. Do you want to talk about it?"

Emily sat on the bed with a huff. "It must be nice to be psychic."

Kaitlin snorted a laugh. "I didn't need psychic powers to tell you were upset downstairs."

"Really?"

She smiled and smoothed a red curl behind her ear. "You yelled at Drew and smacked Holt."

"I did not smack Holt."

"You smacked his hand. When he pointed his finger at you."

"He shouldn't have pointed at me. That was rude."

"Yes. It was." Kaitlin bit back a grin. "And you had every right to smack him. But it was out of character. Also, your aura was all…swirly."

"Swirly?" Emily blinked. "What does that mean? When your aura is swirly?"

Kaitlin fixed her with a steady gaze. "Why don't you tell me?"

"I-I don't know where to start."

"Start at the beginning."

"The part with the dinosaurs?" A pathetic attempt at humor.

Kaitlin was gracious enough to chuckle. "Go back as far as you like."

Emily sighed. "I went for a walk last night, to check out the tide pools and I met him."

"Ash?"

"Mmm hmm." Emily folded her hands in her lap and stared at them as she spoke, anywhere but at Kaitlin's too-knowing eyes. "He invited me for a ride on his Jet Ski. We went to the island and the engine conked out and we had to stay the night in the cabin." She glanced at Kaitlin, who blinked.

"I heard that part already. Why did you talk to him? We had a pact. To avoid those guys like the plague."

"I didn't seek him out. He talked to me first. It was only polite to respond."

Kaitlin tsked. "Your manners are going to bite you in the butt some day."

"Why are you looking at me that way?" Emily knew that look.

"I'm sensing…"

"What?"

"Something different about you. Something…" She shook her head. "I can't put my finger on it."

Emily tipped her chin. She didn't want Kaitlin putting her psychic fingers all over her secrets.

"So he talked to you and you responded because it was polite…"

"And because I liked him. And he seemed nice. So when he invited me out on his Jet Ski, I went."

"And you got stranded at the island. And…" Kaitlin froze. Her lips parted. Her cheeks flushed. And Emily knew, just knew, she'd seen the truth. "Oh, Em."

That was it. Just, "Oh, Em." And a hug.

It was the hug she needed.

"Are you going to be okay?" Kaitlin murmured into her hair.

"I think so."

"Was it… Was it all right?" Of all of them, Kaitlin knew her best. Kaitlin knew her secrets and understood why she avoided men. She'd been the one who had burst in, just as Roman had wrenched up her skirt and ripped off her panties and been about to—

Kaitlin had saved her. And afterwards, Kaitlin had soothed her.

Kaitlin had a gift.

Emily patted her arm. "It was wonderful. It was my choice, Kait. My decision. And I enjoyed every minute of it."

"I'm so glad."

"But..."

"But...what?"

"I'm not sure what happens now. I kind of got the sense he was withdrawing. You know, when we came back. He didn't want to talk about it or hang out together or anything."

She nodded. "Men can be that way. Do you really like him?"

"Yes."

"Then we need to talk to him. To see where he stands. Do you want to go for a walk?"

"Now?"

"Now."

"Okay." And as easily as that, all her rampant emotions settled down. She didn't have a lot of experience with men, but Kaitlin did. She'd know how to handle this. "Thank you, Kaitlin."

They hugged again and Kaitlin laughed.

"What?"

"Bella was right," she said, with a glint in her eye. "You do smell like maple syrup."

He saw her coming and fought back the urge to leap to his feet and run for the hills. He didn't know where that cowardice had come from. Usually when he made up his mind to give a woman the cold shoulder, he had no qualms whatsoever. With Emily, it was different.

He disciplined himself to lean back in the deck chair and pretend to drink his beer as though he hadn't a care in the world. It was a nice day. They'd set up the chairs on the grass in the sun and were diligently getting pleasantly plastered. Despite the fact it wasn't quite noon.

And why the hell not? It was Saturday. It was summertime. He was a wealthy man with no obligations. No responsibilities. Nothing. Whatsoever.

Might as well be drunk.

"Here comes your redhead," Richie muttered. Parker lurched up in his chair.

Devlin lifted the brim of his hat to look. "Hoo mama."

"I can't believe you tapped that," Richie snickered. "You get all the hot pieces of ass."

Parker shot Ash a glare. "You fucked *her*?"

Ash didn't respond. It was none of Parker's business who Ash fucked.

"That blonde is a sweet piece of ass too," Richie said. Ash bit back a growl as something nasty slithered through him.

"Nice rack," Devlin said.

Great. He might have to pound both of them into the ground.

Emily and her friend slowed as they reached his yard. She lifted a hand. "Hey Ash."

Heads whipped around. Parker, Devlin and Richie gaped at him.

"Her?" Richie hissed. "Is she the one?"

Emily winced. Her fingers curled and her hand dropped. She exchanged a glance with her friend, the redhead who looked like she wanted to eviscerate Ash on the spot. Some secret female communication passed between them and the redhead nodded.

"Ash, could we…talk?"

His stomach surged. His pulse pounded. His mouth went dry. "Sure." He set down his beer and stood. God, he hated confrontations. Especially with women. Like this. With their friends standing guard. And his listening in. "What do you want to talk about?"

"I think you know."

"Over here?" He gestured toward the trees and she followed him away from the eavesdropping throng. They stood together in the shade of the evergreens. He crossed his arms over his chest. "What did you want to say?"

Her lips worked. Damn, they were pretty lips. He did not allow himself to be inveigled. Or tempted. Or seduced.

Although he did want to kiss her. Maybe more.

He pushed down that inconvenient desire. One time. One time was his rule. Well, in this case, one night. One tryst. One…whatever it had been.

Regret, and something else, swamped him.

He ignored it. He had to be strong. Resolved. Heartless.

That he wanted her so much, craved just another kiss, should be warning enough. This woman was *dangerous*.

"I was just wondering…" She paused and flicked a glance back at her friend. It made him uncomfortable the way the redhead was watching him. He didn't know why, but it sent shivers up his spine. "I was just wondering what that was between us."

"Between us? It was great. Fucking awesome."

Emily stared at him as though she hadn't understood his words. An uncomfortable silence swelled. Ash felt compelled to fill it. He clenched his teeth to keep his mouth shut.

"Yes. It was awesome. But what was it? I mean, what was it to you?"

"What are you asking?" Hell. He knew what she was asking. But if she wanted her answer, she should fucking ask the right question.

"Was it just a one night stand?"

Aw, shit. She did. She came right out and asked it. And with a wounded, vulnerable expression that skewered him. He steeled his spine. "Probably."

"Probably?" She tipped her head to the side, studying him as though she'd never seen him before.

"Yes."

"Did you take me to that island intending to seduce me there?"

He swallowed. Damn, this was hard. Harder than he'd expected. "Yes."

"And did the engine really conk out?"

He winced. Guilt scalded him. A red tide rose on his cheeks. Something unpleasant prickled at his nape. "No."

Her lips parted and a small breath feathered out. As though someone had punched her in the gut.

"D-did you use me, Ash?"

His throat closed up. He couldn't answer a question like that. No man should ever be expected to.

He was possessed of the sudden urge to defend himself, to tell her his story, explain exactly why he did what he did.

But looking into her eyes, his argument revealed itself for what it was. A weak and self-centered attempt to justify a weak and self-centered existence.

"Did you use me?" she asked again in a soft, low voice.

He couldn't speak. So he nodded.

She paled. Her jaw tightened. Something about her, her light, perhaps, dimmed. "I see. Well." She swallowed. "Thank you for telling me the truth. And...thank you for a lovely evening. I did enjoy—" Her voice broke, halfway through the platitude, as though her good grace had simply worn out. "Goodbye," she said. And she turned and walked away.

He watched her go, feeling oddly like she was taking a piece of him with her.

She passed her friend, and his attention stalled on her. The redhead. Who was watching him. Her face was a mask. When their gazes clashed, something whipped through him. He was certain it was the force of her fury.

But it wasn't fury he saw on her face.

It was pity.

They walked back to the house without a word, for which Emily would be forever grateful. If Kaitlin had said something stupid like, "Are you okay?" she was certain she would burst into tears.

An odd, empty hollow place opened up in her chest as she replayed their conversation again and again, trying to put the pieces together. But her brain didn't want to cooperate. Her heart didn't want to accept the truth.

The beautiful thing she'd thought they'd shared had been nothing but an illusion for her. A game, a conquest, for him.

Kaitlin took her arm when she stumbled over the lip of the yard. She guided Emily to the right, away from the dock where their friends assembled around the boat the guys had brought out. Emily could hear their chattered conversations, their laughter, but as though from a distance. Everything seemed to be at a distance, even her breath.

She stumbled again as they crossed the threshold into the house and again, Kaitlin was there to catch her.

Drew, sitting at the table nibbling on a plate of leftover bacon, glanced up as they entered. As always, his attention snapped to Kaitlin, and Emily was glad for it. She didn't know if she could handle his scrutiny right now. He broke into a grin, which quickly dimmed when he caught the curt shake of Kaitlin's head.

Then his attention lit on Emily. She winced at his expression. "What—" he started, but again Kaitlin silenced him with a look. Without a word, she led Emily up the stairs to her room.

She felt like a zombie. Shuffling, empty, brain dead.

He hadn't wanted her.

He'd only wanted sex.

He'd used her.

As she neared her room, her sanctuary, tears pricked at her lashes. She fought them back. She was a grown woman. She should have seen it. She should have expected it.

She should never have allowed her dreamy fantasies to intrude on a harsh reality.

This is what men were like. This was the way they behaved.

She should have known better.

When the door closed behind her, she could no longer keep her grief at bay. And she didn't care to. She needed to cry. Wail. Mourn.

Kaitlin understood. She wrapped Emily in a tight hug and held her as she wept. Railed at the world, at men, at her own idiocy. It seemed like she cried for hours, but it couldn't have been that long. When she lifted her head, Kaitlin's shoulder was drenched.

"I'm sorry," she snuffled, scrubbing at her cheeks.

"Don't be silly. I'm here for you." Kaitlin thumbed away a stray tear. "I am so sorry, Em."

"I know."

"He's a jerk."

Emily laughed through a sob. "He is. But I thought… I thought…"

"I know." Again, a warm hug.

Which elicited another flurry of weeping. And hugging. And patting.

When Emily was exhausted, when she was completely and utterly drained, she pulled away and murmured, "I thought he was the one. I really really did."

"I know. I know this was a big step for you. Think of it that way, Em.

Did you enjoy it?"

Emily hiccupped. "Yes."

"Then focus on that, darling. Be thankful for that. You had a wonderful first time with a very sexy man. Put him in your rearview mirror and move on."

Move on?

"I...I don't think I can move on."

Kaitlin smiled. It was a sad smile, but one full of love. "I know it hurts right now, but it will get better. I promise. And one day you'll meet a guy who is worthy of you."

"I was so sure..."

A strange look flickered over Kaitlin's face. "I know. I know you thought he was the one, but—"

"Did you?"

Kaitlin blanched. Pressed her lips together.

"Did you?"

"You know I don't read my friends. My own hopes for them, my own expectations get in the way."

"Right. But when you met him, did you think he was the one for me? Or was I just imagining this sense of...rightness?" Emily tugged on Kaitlin's hand. "Please. I need to know."

Kaitlin sighed. Her lashes fluttered. It was clear she did not want to answer.

Emily tugged again. "Please."

"All right. Yes. Okay? Yes. I thought he was the one for you." And then a flush rose on her cheeks.

Because Kaitlin was rarely mistaken about something like that.

But this time she too had gotten it wrong.

Somehow that gave Emily a tiny bit of comfort.

She wasn't the only one he'd fooled.

CHAPTER EIGHT

The rest of the weekend was a bust. Both Parker and Devlin disappeared for the better part of Saturday, leaving Ash alone with Richie. Then Richie got swimmingly drunk that night and started a fight at the bar by grabbing Bella Cross when she came out of the ladies' room and shoving his hand between her legs.

What an idiot. Bella was Holt Lamm's girlfriend, and Holt didn't take any shit off anybody.

None of them did. Not Holt. Not Cam Jackson. Not Drew Boone.

After Holt decked Richie, the three of them all turned and glared at Ash, bristling, fists flexing, as though they wanted to do the same to him.

So when Darby suggested he and Richie leave, and *tout de suite*, they complied. He tromped back to his house, supporting Richie's staggering weight, and got drunk—well, drunker—there.

On Sunday, he stayed on his deck and watched his neighbors take turns running their speedboat. He caught a glimpse of Bella, the redhead and a brunette. But there was no sign of Emily, and he was glad. He wasn't looking for her. He didn't want to see her again. He didn't.

It was bad enough that every time he closed his eyes he could see her wounded expression. At night he awoke in a sweat with a raging hard on, thinking about her. He pushed her from his mind, brutally evicting any and all memories, fantasies, ridiculous hopes. And somehow, she kept slipping back in.

It was damned annoying.

He had a rule. He lived by his rule. It had never bothered him before.

Why did it haunt him now?

When he and the guys boarded the home-bound ferry, Holt and Cam and all of them were already camped in the corner booth. Emily was with them, but surrounded, as though they were protecting her.

Not that it mattered. He didn't want to talk to her or see her.

Ever.

Every time he so much as thought of her, the gap in his soul opened up a little more, letting in the cold, howling wind.

On Monday, his mother called to cancel dinner…and to let him know she was leaving for Monaco and, by the way, she was divorcing George and probably marrying Rafael.

Ash pretended the news of her newest impending divorce didn't launch him into an even deeper depression. His mother had married and divorced more men than he could remember. At one point, he'd kept a spreadsheet, but then, after number eight—or had it been number nine?—he'd realized it was a pointless effort.

Some people just couldn't stay married.

He hated that he was one of them.

On Wednesday, his father called and invited him to dinner. His first inclination was to cry off. He wasn't in the mood to be civilized, but Dad had insisted. *They had news,* he warned.

Ash was certain he knew what it was.

And damn. He liked Michelle.

She was a bit young for Dad, but she was a nice person. He'd really hoped *their* marriage would work out.

He'd spent his life living in two homes with revolving doors. One spouse out, another in. By now, he should know better. He should have expected the romantic bubble Dad and Michelle had been frolicking in would burst sooner or later.

It always did.

He drove up the driveway to the mansion with a ball in his belly and a nice bottle of Grenache cradled in the passenger seat of his M6. What kind of wine did one take to a divorce? He wished he knew. By now he should know. He hopped out and tossed Vickers the keys to his BMW. Holding the wine bottle by the neck he stepped into the expansive foyer and nodded to Halsey.

"They are in the small sitting room," the butler intoned. Ash nodded and headed down the hall. He paused at the open door to the intimate parlor, taking in the scene. It was just family, Dad and Michelle on the loveseat, his sister Trish and her husband Sal on the sofa and Effie on the floor at their feet, sucking on her fingers. Sam was building a house of cards on the coffee table, explaining physics in a pedantic tone.

Sam was pretty pedantic, for a seven-year-old. He glanced up and saw Ash, and waved madly. Then he slapped his forehead as the tower of cards came crashing down. "Dang," he howled.

"You can build it up again, little man," Dad said, clapping him on the back.

Dad did that a lot. Clapped them on the back, his sons. Built them back up again.

But Ash didn't feel like anyone could build him back up again. Not after the week he'd had.

"Ash." Michelle met him at the door with a kiss to his cheek. She was pretty and petite, but a force to be reckoned with. He didn't envy his father the battle to come. He attempted a smile as he handed her the wine. She grinned. "Oh, thank you. My favorite."

"Hey Ash," Trish blew him a kiss. Apparently she couldn't bear to be separated from Sal enough to come say hello. Now those two were in love. Had been since the day they'd met. His sister hadn't even wanted Ash to do a background check on the guy.

He had of course.

Sal had passed. Squeaky clean. He was a cop for a local small city. He did charity work. And his family had old money. When Ash had asked him why he was a cop when his family was richer than shit, Sal had laughed and said something about making the world a better place.

At the time, Ash hadn't understood what he meant by that. Donating money and supporting charities did make the world a better place. It was only recently that he'd been itching, aching, wanting more in what now seemed like a pointless life.

But he didn't want to be a cop.

"Sit down. Sit down," Dad said, after pulling him into a long hug. "Everyone's here. Now we can share our news." He and Michelle exchanged a glance. "Do you want to tell them, or should I?"

Ash steeled himself.

"I want to tell them." Michelle glowed.

His brow knit in confusion. Why would this announcement make her so damned happy? Unless she was getting a huge settlement?

"We—" She shot a beatific look around the room. "We're pregnant."

Ash's jaw dropped.

Dad nodded madly, and grinning like a loon. "Yup. We're pregnant."

"Oh Dad." Trish jumped to her feet and wrapped them both in a huge hug. "Congratulations."

"Congratulations." Sal shook Dad's hand.

Ash mimicked the actions, but it was as though he reached out through a long dark tunnel.

His father was having another baby.

His mother was getting a divorce and maybe marrying Rafael.

And there was Ash, caught in limbo, in the middle of nowhere. A no-man's land. Alone.

Forever.

Why Emily's face flickered through his mind just then, he had no idea.

* * * * *

"I don't like seeing you like this, son," Dad said.

Ash turned away from the window, where he'd been staring at the darkness, out into the yard toward the tree house they'd built when he'd been ten. He'd been so lost in thought he hadn't heard his father come up behind him.

"I'm fine."

"Really?" Those eyes, so like his own, resonated skepticism. "You don't seem fine."

Ash sighed. "Mother's getting another divorce."

"Ah."

Ash raked his fingers through his hair. "I don't know why it surprised me."

"Sandra was always…a restless spirit."

"It just…I don't know, validates my lack of faith in marriage." All over again.

"Marriage isn't a thing independent of us, Ash. It's a relationship between two people. Each marriage is different. Driven by the participants. It can be whatever you want it to be."

"But there are two people involved. That's the sticking point. You can never trust the other person's motives."

"No. You can't. Sometimes you have to go on faith."

"Every time I've done that, I got burned."

"Not all women are like your mother. Or Jillian." Ash winced at his ex-wife's name. "There are good women out there."

Ash snorted. "Like Teresa?"

"You haven't had the best luck. That doesn't mean you quit trying."

"Doesn't it?"

"You've gotta kiss a lot of frogs…"

"Frogs? Really Dad?"

Dad grinned. "You know what I mean. You weren't meant to spend your life alone, son. None of us were."

"I'd rather be alone than go through that pain again."

"Because there's no pain whatsoever in being alone."

Ash glared at his father, not appreciating the sarcasm.

"I got lucky with Michelle. We love each other deeply. And completely. But Ash, it wasn't an easy road for me. There were some missteps along the way."

"Was Mother one of those missteps?"

"I loved her. I did. But we are better apart. It was better for *you* for us to separate. Trust me on that." Ash didn't respond. He couldn't see how that could be true. When his parents had split, he'd been devastated. "And even though it didn't work out in the end, I can't regret being with her. I wouldn't change that decision for the world. Because it brought me you. I feel the same about Elaine and June." Trish's and Sam's mothers. Yeah, Dad had been through a litany of wives. He was hardly someone to give advice. That didn't stop him. "Sometimes you gotta take risks."

Ash swallowed a laugh. "Don't let Bradley hear you say that." Their family lawyer was all about risk mitigation.

"At the end of the day, whose face are you going to see in the mirror? Bradley's?" Dad chuckled. "Because that would be a bad day." Bradley was a surly old coot. "My point is this, Ash. When you're my age, and you're looking back at your life, what kind of landscape do you want to see?"

Ash turned away. A band tightened around his chest.

"Do you want it to be filled with love and warmth and children, and maybe sprinkled with a regret or two? Or do you want it to be pristine and sanitized and sterile? Because that's the kind of choice you're facing right now."

Ash blanched. "What do you mean?" Could his father know? Read his inner turmoil?

"You're nearly thirty, Ash."

"What's that supposed to mean?"

Dad sighed. "Nothing. But I was thirty once. Yesterday." He glanced over at the sofa, where Trish dandled his granddaughter on her knee. "Life passes pretty quickly, son. We think we have all the time in the world, and then one day, we wake up and realize we missed it. Missed so much."

Something unpleasant coiled in Ash's gut. "What are you saying, Dad?"

"I'm planning to retire."

Shock rippled, making his vision blur. "What?"

"The corporation is run by the board for the most part, but I'd like you to start taking over the reins of the foundation."

"Dad...are you... Is everything okay?" He seemed healthy as a horse, but sometimes you could never tell.

"I'm fine. Fine. Really I am. Well, a little high blood pressure and some diverticulitis, but you don't want to hear about that. It's just, with Michelle and the baby coming... Trish and Effie. I want to spend more time with the people I love." He gazed at them, there by the fire, his love in his eyes. "So, will you? Take over some of the foundation responsibilities?"

"I..." Warmth flooded Ash's veins. He had trouble forming the words. This was what he needed. This was what he'd been searching for. A chance to make a difference. A chance to do something that mattered. Something beyond his art. "I would be honored."

It could have been a meaningful moment. A bonding between father and son. The passing of the torch. But Dad just chortled, slapped him on the shoulder and said, "Great. I'll have my secretary shoot you a list of upcoming events."

Ash had the sneaking suspicion he'd just been played.

And somehow, he didn't care.

Michelle called them all into the dining room then and Ash enjoyed a lively dinner surrounded by his family. The conversation as the courses were served was engaging and funny and it warmed that cold place in his heart. It was quite a departure from his typical lonely meals in his penthouse apartment, and he found himself wondering why he didn't do this more often. He loved his father and his siblings. Heck, he even loved Michelle.

And Dad was right. Life was short. He should spend more time with the people he loved.

Sal had just cracked a joke that had them all in stitches when Ash looked at his father and stilled. Foreboding prickled at his nape.

As laughter wreathed the room, along with the sounds of cutlery and chatter, Adam Bristol went white. Confusion flickered over his face and he stood, gripping his left arm. He opened his mouth, but no words came out. Nothing but a muffled groan.

And then he fell to the floor.

CHAPTER NINE

There was nothing to do. Nothing to do but wait. Ash impatiently checked his Rolex and growled when it was only thirty seconds later than the last time he'd checked it. He repressed the urge to leap to his feet and charge to the nurses' station and demand information, because they hadn't known anything two minutes ago. They probably didn't know anything more now.

He glanced at Michelle, who was huddled with Trish in a bank of seats by the window. Cold coffee in Styrofoam cups sat before them on the table. Sal had taken Effie and Sam home for the night. Between them, they'd tried to convince Trish and Michelle to go get some sleep, with no luck.

Honestly, Ash couldn't blame them. There was this sense—sitting in the sterilized waiting room listening to nurses' shoes squeak on the floor and wincing at the disembodied tones announcing a "Code Blue"—that if one left, it would give disaster the opportunity to move in.

It was an illogical notion. Ash was the guardian, the protector, of nothing.

As he sat and waited, he stewed. He thought about what his father had said to him, a mere hour before he'd collapsed, and he wondered…would that be the last conversation they ever shared?

"Sometimes you have to take risks, son. When you're looking back at your life, what kind of landscape do you want to see?"

What did he want? He knew he wasn't satisfied with the way his life was now.

Which was ludicrous.

He could do anything he wanted. Have anything he wanted.

But there was a problem with a life like that. It lacked structure. It certainly lacked meaning. When he woke up in the morning, he had no plan whatsoever but to please himself.

He should be happier than a pig in shit.

But he wasn't.

He ached.

And that emptiness, well, it echoed inside him.

Sure, he had his friends. He had a great family. He had hobbies and cars and, for fuck's sake, a Rolex. But deep, deep down, he had nothing.

Deep, deep down, he was utterly alone.

And he was damn tired of it.

Why Emily's face popped into his mind just then was a mystery. Thankfully, it wasn't a vision of her expression when he'd told her the brutal truth, exposed his dark heart. It was the memory of her wonder as she gazed up at those eagles, perched high in the pines, calling to their mates.

Her delight had shone through her eyes. Burned into him. Searing him. Branding him with an indelible mark.

When he thought of her, the ache, the hole in his heart, eased.

He did not know why.

So as he waited on the uncomfortable plastic chair, sipping stone-cold and bitter coffee, waiting for news he wasn't sure he wanted to hear, he thought of her. Just the peace. Just for the comfort. More than he should have. He thought about the way she found joy in little things, like the slant of the sun through the trees, or the smell of brewing coffee or the brush of his lips. He thought about her smile, her sincerity, her open acceptance. Her trust.

Her reaction when he'd admitted to using her haunted him. He couldn't help thinking he'd held something amazing in his hand, and crumpled it and tossed it away.

She could have been the one, he realized in a plunging epiphany. She could have been the one, and he'd ruined it.

The nurse finally came out to tell them Dad had been stabilized, but, with the exception of his wife, couldn't see visitors until the morning. So Ash and Trish continued to wait in the echoing and empty holding pen, huffing antiseptic, until Michelle emerged.

She was weepy and shaken, but reported that Adam was doing much better. And he would like them all to return tomorrow. Relief nearly brought him to his knees.

But Michelle wasn't finished yet. Her voice wavered as she shared the real news. Adam Bristol was slated for surgery at noon.

The doctors were hopeful he would survive.

Ash's head buzzed.

Hopeful. They were *hopeful* he would survive.

Somehow that didn't feel like very hopeful news at all.

And it hit him. Hit him hard.

Tomorrow, he might lose his dad.

He didn't sleep at all that night. He tossed and turned and thought about his father, and the good times they'd had. Surf fishing on the coast, traveling through India together on that business trip when Dad had been between wives. Building that tree house with Parker. He remembered when Sam was born. Remembered watching his dad hold him for the first time, looking down at his tiny face as though he represented a miracle, a salvation.

Ash hadn't understood at the time, and wasn't sure he ever would understand the emotion behind Dad's expression that day. It killed him that the new baby, Michelle's baby, might never know its father.

And then, for some reason, deep in the dark of night, when he was giddy from exhaustion and worry and half-adrift on the sea of slumber, another vision visited him.

It was a terrifying vision, but fascinating too.

This time Ash was the father. He cradled a tiny, helpless bundle in his arms, looking down at that precious little person, his heart swelling with pride and joy and…adoration. He glanced up at *her*, the woman who made this miracle, made him whole, and she smiled. A balm on an aching soul. Love shone from those icy blue eyes. "Ash…" she whispered. It was Emily's voice.

He snapped awake. Shot up in the bed. Clutched his chest.

Holy God.

It came to him like a thunderclap.

That was what he wanted.

The dream haunted him the rest of the day.

Ash was relieved to be able to visit his father before the surgery, although it shocked him to see the man he admired and respected, above everyone else in the world, laid flat on his back and connected to a tangle of tubes and beeping machines. He seemed…diminished.

The wait during the surgery was dreadful, though Parker, bless him, came by to wait with him. And he brought a deck of cards. They all whiled away the hours playing poker and spades, but when Trish suggested gin rummy, Ash made an excuse to leave and wandered off to the cafeteria. Because gin rummy made him think of *her*.

Though Parker came with him, they didn't talk. They didn't need to talk.

They got coffee, though neither wanted it, and sat at a booth in the corner.

"How you holding up?" Parker asked.

Ash shrugged. Sipped. Grimaced. "Okay I guess."

"He'll be fine. I'm sure."

"Yeah."

"Your dad is strong as a bull."

"Yeah." Ash didn't dare let doubt creep in. He couldn't bear it.

Silence descended. They both brooded, surrounded by their own cloud of worry. It was nice, he realized, to have someone with whom no mindless chatter was necessary.

But one thing needed to be said. "Thank you for being here, Parker."

"Of course. He, ah…" Parker flushed, making the scar on his neck stand out. Ash hardly even noticed it any more. To him Parker was just…Parker. "Your dad…means the world to me."

Ash nodded and took another sip of his coffee, though he didn't want it. When Parker had been a boy, the victim of an appalling crime, Ash's father had taken him under his wing. Adam was as much a father to Parker as he was to Ash himself.

Yeah. It was damn comforting to have someone there. Someone who understood.

It was hours and hours, and gallons of truly awful coffee, before the nurse announced Adam was out of surgery, and hours more before she permitted them to see him.

Ash was annoyed to the gills that Parker wasn't allowed into the ICU. Because he wasn't family. But he was.

"How you doin', Dad?" Ash asked, gingerly taking his hand. It was disconcertingly cold.

Adam forced a smile, but it was more like a grimace. "Feel like I've been chewed up and spit out."

Trish patted his arm, careful not to dislodge the IV. "Open heart surgery will do that to you, Dad."

Michelle raked back his hair and pressed a kiss on his forehead. "The doctors said it went well. You'll be home within a week."

"A week?"

She waggled a finger at him. "No complaints. You'll do everything those nurses tell you, you hear? I want you home, safe and sound. And I want you healthy." She set her palm to her belly, and the two exchanged a meaningful glance. "Your daughter needs you to be healthy."

"A daughter?" Adam croaked. And then, "You weren't supposed to tell me."

Michelle offered a watery grin. "You need to know, Adam. You need to think about her and how much she will need her father. This sweet little angel."

The nurse squeaked in to shoo them out. "He needs his rest," she announced like an Admiral through a bullhorn.

But before Ash could leave, Dad caught his arm. "Take care of her, Ash. If anything happens," he whispered. "Take care of them all."

He couldn't manage a response. Nothing more than a nod.

His throat was too damn swollen to speak.

The next week Dad came home from the hospital and Ash finally felt like he could breathe again. The wait had been excruciating. He spent that time with his family, almost exclusively. Hanging out with Sam, taking his brother and stepmother to the hospital to visit his dad, then squiring them around the local malls as Michelle succumbed to what she called her "nesting instinct." A month ago he would have been mortified to stand outside a Nordstrom's dressing room holding her purse while she tried on clothes. Now all he cared about was that she was looking for an outfit to welcome his father home.

During that time, he tried not to think about Emily, but she kept creeping into his mind. He woke up thinking about her and went to sleep every night regretting his actions.

He ignored the growing panic.

Panic that he'd missed the boat.

He tried to expunge her, but apparently there wasn't enough alcohol in the world. In the end, he had to admit, he'd made a monumental mistake.

Typically, Ash wasn't the kind of guy to make mistakes. That was probably why it took him so long to figure it out. To realize what this pain in his chest meant whenever he thought of her. He was sure it wasn't love—it couldn't be love—but it was something. Guilt, probably. He knew he wouldn't be at peace again, until he saw her. Maybe apologized for being a dick.

And he had been a dick.

He saw that now.

He'd been a dick most of his life.

So he would find her and apologize and maybe give her something pretty, like diamonds. In his experience, women liked diamonds. They absolved a multitude of sins. If that went well, he would ask her out on a date and woo her or something.

He'd never had to woo a woman before and he wasn't sure what that entailed, but he was sure he could figure it out.

If she would even talk to him.

Which she probably wouldn't.

He had no idea what he would do then.

When he went to visit his favorite jewelry store to pick up a bauble, his attention stalled on a brilliant marquis diamond ring. He felt like an idiot buying it. The only woman he might give it to probably hated him.

But he bought it. Hell, it was only money.

It felt right, that weight in his pocket. Comforting. It would be his totem. His inspiration. The reminder of what he really wanted in life.

Whether or not he could have it with her.

Hell, he didn't know if he could find her, much less get her to listen to his apology. But he had to try. He just couldn't rest until he did…something.

When he couldn't reach Lane, he called a friend who was a private investigator and, armed only with the information he had, that her name was Emily and she taught third grade, asked Danny to help him find her. It took Danny less than an hour to search the school databases and report back that there were thirty-four Emilys teaching school in Washington State, and eight of those taught third grade.

Only eight.

Excellent.

He could visit each of those schools and find her. It wouldn't take very long.

Ash was over the moon with the information, until Danny reminded him it was summer.

He went to the island that weekend, hoping she'd be there. He didn't even know her last name, didn't even know where to find her if she wasn't at the house next to his.

She wasn't there.

But her guardians were.

Lane Daniels, Holt Lamm and—horrors—Bella Cross sat on the dock. As Ash walked up, they all glared at him. Bella, sitting on the planks with Holt by her side, kicked up a spray of water at the sight of him.

"Bristol." Lane nodded coolly. Apparently, his friends had brought him up to date on what had happened between Ash and Emily. The others said nothing. An uncomfortable silence sizzled.

"Do, ah, you have a minute?"

Lane threw out his hands, embracing the expansive horizon. "I've got all day."

Ash shot a glance around the dock. Shivered. "I was hoping to talk to you in private."

Brows arched. All of them. Practically in tandem. *"Really?"* they said.

"It's kind of important."

A growl resonated from Bella's throat.

Holt leaned over and kissed her on the forehead. "Bella, honey, would you go up to the house and get me another beer?"

Bella frowned, but then she caught Holt's expression. Something flickered on her face. "Oh, all right," she muttered, and rose. He smacked her gently on the ass and received, incomprehensibly, a grin from her.

"Thanks babe."

Ash knew Holt had sent Bella away because he didn't want her to witness what was coming. A shitstorm of gargantuan proportions. He steeled his spine. He deserved it. He knew it.

But both Holt and Lane at the same time? He didn't think he could handle that. "I was hoping to talk to Lane," he said.

"Yeah," Holt smiled. It was a chilling smile. His muscles rippled as he flexed. "But I got something to say to you."

"Look, I know I was an ass…" Okay. Maybe he shouldn't have said anything.

Holt bounded to his feet and towered over him and hissed, "Ass doesn't begin to cover it. You have no idea."

Ash didn't understand what Holt meant by that, but it didn't matter too much. The overall vibe was pretty clear. Especially when he added, "Keep away from Emily, Ash. She's way too good for you." He started to storm away, as though he had to, or he'd lose control and do violence or something, but then he stopped in his tracks and whirled around. "If I hear that you so much as talked to that girl, I'll rip out your throat." Then Holt whirled on his heel and marched up the hill to the house.

"He means it." Why Lane said it with a chuckle was a mystery. It wasn't funny, the prospect of being torn to shreds by a guy like Holt Lamm.

"No doubt."

"So? You wanted to talk to me? Better spit it out. Because Bella may be back soon and if you thought Holt was scary…"

Jesus. Who knew one girl would have so many fanatical champions? Though Ash understood how Emily inspired such fierce loyalty.

She was something special.

Ash waved at the deck chair next to Lane's. "May I?" Normally he would never ask for permission to sit, but instinctively, he knew he had to be on his best behavior if he was going to get what he needed from Lane.

"Be my guest." An icy tone.

Ash sat, but hardly knew where to start. "I…ah… My divorce was bad."

Lane grunted.

"And there were a few other…unpleasant situations with women I got involved with. They were all only after money. So…I made a vow. One time with a woman. One time only. No relationships. Certainly not with a woman like Emily."

"A woman like her?"

"You know." The word clogged his throat. God it sounded pompous. "Poor."

Lane laughed.

"What?"

"Nothing." Lane glanced at him then. "How's that lone wolf thing working out for you?"

Heat crept up Ash's cheeks. "Guys in our situation…We have to be careful. You of all people should understand."

Lane bristled. "Lucy's nothing like Jillian. And Em? She's one of the good ones too. If she loved you, it would be for who you are, not your money. I guaran-fucking-tee it."

Now, when he looked back, he could see it. Her joy in the simple things. Her wide-eyed innocence, her purity of spirit.

Emily was not a gold digger.

"So, why are you telling me all this, Ash? What do you want?"

"I just want to talk to her. Explain." Beg for forgiveness, maybe.

"Okay. What's the problem?"

"I don't know how to reach her. Hell, I don't even know her last name." Another laugh. Why Lane found this so amusing, he didn't know. "Can you give me her number?"

"Are you insane?"

Ash set his teeth. "I need to talk to her."

"I think you've said enough." Lane's nose wrinkled, as though he couldn't stand the sight of Ash's face. "She truly liked you. Too bad you fucked it up. Now she wants nothing to do with you."

"I miss her. I really miss her."

"Yeah. I'll bet you do. I'm not giving you her number."

"How about her name?"

Surely he would condescend to that tiny crumb.

But no. His expression made that more than clear.

"I will find her. I will find her and apologize. If I have to haunt this island every weekend."

"Do what you gotta do. But you're not getting her contact info from me, dude. And if you do find her?" Hope flickered in his chest at the thought. "And you hurt her again? I guarantee, Holt will kill you."

Ash's smile was watery. "What if Holt's not around?"

"Then I'll kill you." With that, Lane—a guy who'd been his loyal friend for ten years—sprang from the deck chair, snatched up his towel and stormed away, leaving Ash feeling shredded. And defeated. And alone.

CHAPTER TEN

"There." Emily sighed as she glanced around the ballroom. It was beautiful, elegantly decorated. Everything was in place. From the silent auction items along the far wall to the exquisite table settings, to the band finishing their final sound check on the stage. Pride swelled in her chest. It meant so much that she had the resources and abilities to pull off a charity event like this. And it comforted her to know that, even if her own fairy tale would never come true, she could help someone else have theirs. "I think it's perfect."

"Of course it's perfect," Kaitlin grinned, hugging her shoulder. "You're a slave driver."

Emily wrinkled her nose. "Am I?"

Jamie snorted. "Are you kidding? When it comes to events like this, you become practically militant."

Emily nibbled her lip. "I'm sorry…"

"Don't be sorry. You're good at this, Em. Really good."

"Yeah." Jamie crossed her arms and surveyed the room, watching the rest of the volunteers make final adjustments to the balloon arches. "We are going to make so much money for the Teen Waystation, it's not even funny."

"I hope so." This was one of Emily's favorite causes. No one should be homeless, but when teens, kids just starting out in life, found themselves alone in the world, something had to be done. Someone had to step in. Some of their stories were heartbreaking.

It had been such a relief over the past two weeks, having this event to occupy her time. Her mind. She'd been too busy to think about Ash. Well, until nighttime. When she lay in her bed, staring at the ceiling blinking back the tears.

Which was foolish. He'd made his position clear.

Theirs had been a one night stand. He had no interest in anything else.

She'd been so sure the feeling she had when she was with him was real. That *they* were real. But then, she kept reminding herself, it wasn't as though she was experienced in things like this.

It was her own fault.

After one near-disastrous interaction with a man in college, she'd erected very thick, firm and impenetrable walls. She hadn't dated. She hadn't trusted. Hadn't even paddled in the pond. Had she truly imagined she could just dive in and swim like a fish?

It was simply ironic that the first time she let down her guard it was to a man who wanted only one thing.

Or maybe it wasn't ironic.

Maybe she just had really poor taste in men.

Which only validated her vow to give up on men.

Or relationships.

Or, at the very least, impulsive decisions.

Like leaping into bed with a man she barely knew and expecting him to respect her in the morning.

Her stomach churned and she tried to calm it with a palm. It didn't help. Her stomach had been churning a lot lately.

"Ooh, look." Jamie waylaid a waiter carrying a tray of champagne to the welcome area and grabbed three glasses. She handed one to Kaitlin and another to Emily. "A toast. To a successful fund-raiser."

Emily raised her glass, but before she could take a sip, Kaitlin touched her wrist. "I don't think you should drink," she murmured.

Emily blinked. "What? Why?" But Kaitlin just fixed her with that crooked, unfocused stare and shook her head.

"No alcohol."

It was damned annoying having a friend who was privy to the secrets of the universe and wouldn't spill the beans. But Kaitlin was nearly always right, so Emily asked the waiter for a club soda instead. Besides, she had a lot of work to do before the night was over.

The true reason for Kaitlin's insistence became clear before long. Halfway through the lively event, Jamie, at her side, bristled. "What's *he* doing here?" she spat.

Emily followed her glare and her breath seized as her focus landed on an achingly familiar face.

Ash.

He was here.

She'd considered not sending an invitation to the Bristol Foundation, but they had always been generous benefactors in the past. In the end, she'd decided against letting her petty feelings stand between the Teen Waystation and a large cash infusion. Besides, Ash had never actually attended a fund-raiser. It had always been his father or one of the other Directors.

She was shocked to see him here.

A part of her wanted to run and hide. She told that part to shush.

This was her event. Her world. She'd be damned if she'd let him chase her back into her hidey-hole. She'd spent enough of her life in that cave, isolated from the world.

That was over now.

Her gaze flicked to the man Ash was talking to and her gut clenched. Her breath stalled. Her heart lodged in her throat.

Kaitlin laid a hand on her arm. "Are you okay?"

"Mmm hmm."

But she wasn't. Because the two men in the world she least wanted to see, ever again, were chatting amiably by the bar. Ash said something and Roman threw back his head and laughed.

Roman.

He was tall, lean, handsome. The years showed on his features, but that silky charisma, the charm that had trapped her once, had not faded. He turned in her direction and he froze, drink halfway to his lips. He looked her up and down and they curled then, those lips. The mask slipped, just a tiny bit, and his true nature showed through the cracks.

Fairy tales might not be true, but ogres did exist, and Roman was one.

"He's coming this way."

Emily didn't need Jamie's warning. Her survival instinct snapped to attention as Roman headed toward her, a predatory glint in his eye. Ash didn't follow. Thank God. He hadn't even noticed her.

Regardless, the urge to run hit her again, and hit her hard.

Ash glanced up then and their gazes clashed. His muscles tightened. Some unfamiliar expression flickered over his features and he started making his way across the room as well.

"Oh God." She swallowed.

"We're here." God bless Kaitlin. She always knew what to say.

It helped, a lot, having her friends at her back. Because her worst nightmare was heading toward her, and Ash Bristol wasn't far behind. She wasn't sure which encounter she dreaded more.

Society events like this had never been Ash's thing. Pressing the flesh, talking to overblown socialites, forcing himself to smile and be charming to complete strangers—all of whom knew *him*—set his teeth on edge.

It had been a relief at first, seeing Roman Carstairs' familiar face at the fund-raiser, the first one he'd agreed to take on in his father's stead. But it hadn't taken long for Ash to remember how much he disliked the man. But they were fraternity brothers, and this was a charity event, so Ash disciplined himself to be civil.

It rankled, laughing at his jokes and making small talk. Roman had a crude sense of humor, and didn't shy away from making rude comments about the people around them. He seemed to know everyone, and all their dirty little secrets, so when he chuckled and said, "There's someone I want to talk to," Ash had nodded and turned away.

And then he'd seen her. His heart had thudded painfully. Breathing became difficult. Prickles of heat rose on his nape.

Emily.

He'd found her.

Some unfamiliar joy trilled through him.

And then annoyance raked him when he realized *she* was the one Roman was heading for.

She was impossibly beautiful in a light green gown that clung to her curves. Her hair was done up in some elaborate swirly confection; the touch of lipstick snagged his attention, making him imagine those lips engaged in more intimate pursuits.

She was dazzling in purple overalls and a floppy hat. All dolled up like this, she was irresistible.

As he and Roman approached, her muscles stiffened infinitesimally. A veil shrouded her eyes. She hummed with a tension that reached out and grabbed him by the balls, and not in a good way.

He knew he'd hurt her. He just hadn't realized how badly.

Seeing it, feeling it, nearly destroyed him.

Because he realized, his lame idea of simply apologizing and handing over some sparkly bauble wasn't going to be nearly enough. If he wanted to win her back, he was going to have to do much, much more.

Although what that might be, he didn't know.

"Emily." Roman greeted her with an effusive hug. She stared at Ash over his shoulder as he rocked her back and forth. The agony on her delicate features hurt. Like a knife to the gut. When Roman finally let her go, she seemed to shrink inside herself. She threw her shoulders back and plastered an enormous smile on her face.

It was, patently, the fakest smile he'd ever seen.

He didn't like it at all. It wasn't...*her.*

"It's been a long time." Roman turned to Emily's companions and winced. They were both bristling, like soldiers readying for war, wary glowers flicking from him to Roman and back again. "Kaitlin." Roman held out a hand. The redhead's lip curled. So when Roman greeted the brunette with the short bangs, he didn't bother trying. He merely nodded. "Jamie."

"Roman." This she spat. "What are you doing here?"

Roman laughed and waved to a waiter, grabbing another flute of champagne, though he'd already had three—that Ash had counted. "I had to come…when I heard our Emily was organizing the event." His expression became overly sincere. "Oh and because I really really care about…" He glanced at Ash. "What's this a fund-raiser for again?"

Ash cleared his throat. "Teen Waystation."

"Yeah. Teen Waystation." Roman threw back his drink and snagged another. "Obesity is a terrible problem in our society."

Emily made a sound, something like a snort.

"Teen Waystation is a homeless shelter." Ash knew. He'd read the prospectus before deciding the amount the foundation would give. Now, however, he wished he'd written the check for more. He shook his head and his gaze tangled with Emily's. She appeared torn between outrage and bemusement. She opted for politeness.

"Thank you very much for coming, Roman. I hope you have a wonderful evening."

It appeared then, that she intended to slip away. Denial howled. He couldn't let her go. Not now that he'd found her again. He opened his mouth to forestall her, but Roman beat him to it.

"Do you know Ash Bristol?" he asked. "From the Bristol Foundation?"

Emily nodded graciously in his direction. "I believe we've met."

Ash thrust out a hand because he knew she would take it. She couldn't not in a situation like this. Her manners would not allow her to give him the direct cut in a crowd of wealthy donors. It was a sleazy way to get to touch her, but Ash had few regrets, because when her palm slid across his, a dizzying sensation assailed him. And he remembered.

Oh, he'd always remembered. He'd remembered it all. But this was more. This was sensory memory. His body recognized her touch and delighted, exalted in it. The moment lasted forever, and not nearly long enough.

Also, her friends were glaring at him. So he released her. But he didn't step back. He liked being near her too much. He wished he could whisk her away to some darkened, private room and—

His brain seized as images flickered through.

And *talk* to her. Talk to her. He brutally reminded himself that he needed to talk to her. Explain. Apologize. Grovel. He would find a way to get her alone. Tonight. And talk to her.

"So, I hear you have an item up in the auction?" Roman asked.

Emily blinked. "Y-yes."

He leaned closer, way too close in Ash's opinion, and whispered, "I'll have to win that."

She glanced at her friends, anxiety flickering in her eyes.

Ash shot a look at Roman. And then at Emily. He wasn't a terribly observant guy in social situations, but there was something between these two. Roman made Emily ill at ease.

On the one hand, Ash was relieved the discomfort he'd sensed from her wasn't totally directed at him. On the other hand, he knew Roman. That he and Emily had a *history*, bothered him.

"What item did you offer?" he asked. "One of your glass pieces?"

All of them, Emily, Roman, Kaitlin and Jamie, gaped.

"Glass pieces?" Kaitlin's head whipped around. She narrowed her attention on Emily. "What glass pieces?"

She flushed. "No. No. Of course not. My art's not nearly sophisticated enough to offer at an auction."

"I didn't know you did art," Kaitlin said. "Why didn't I know you did art?" She frowned at Ash, but it was softened by a contemplative light.

"It's just a silly hobby." Emily waved a hand, as though she could brush the topic away. "No, my item in the auction is a fundraising package."

Jamie selected a rumaki from a passing tray. "She'll coordinate an event for the winning bidder."

Emily's flush rose. Ash found himself fascinated by the tinge on her cheeks. "It's nothing really."

"I'll have to win that." Roman repeated. "Then you and I could spend hours and hours together on…you know. Some fundraising event."

Ash disliked the tightness around her mouth at that. No. He wasn't terribly observant, but he was intuitive enough to know Emily did not want to spend hours and hours with Roman. And if he knew Roman, he knew why.

At the same time, the thought of spending hours and hours—alone—with Emily excited him beyond reason. He decided then and there, no matter how much Roman bid for Emily's package, Ash was going to win it.

CHAPTER ELEVEN

Emily nearly fainted with relief when Joann signaled it was time for her to give her speech. She nodded politely at Ash and Roman and, hooking arms with Kaitlin and Jamie said, "Excuse us, gentlemen."

It seemed as though Roman was going to follow, but Ash asked him some question, distracting him long enough for her to slip away. She blew out a breath.

"You did great." Kaitlin patted her hand. "That can't have been easy."

"I would have smacked one of them," Jaime muttered. "Or both of them."

"It's over now," Emily said. She gored Kaitlin with a dark look. "I need you to haunt that auction table. Top any bid Roman lays down. I'll cover it. Will you do that for me?"

"You know I will."

After her speech, Emily made the rounds from table to table, chatting with the guests and sharing why Teen Waystation was such an important cause. She saw Ash milling in the crowd, mingling with representatives from some of the other foundations. But every time he approached her, she quickly found someone else to talk to, even if it was a volunteer or a waiter or random stranger. The same strategy worked with Roman, but she had to be more vigilant, because he was far sneakier.

Kaitlin was manning the silent auction table and Jamie was covering the donations table, so neither of them could offer any help.

It stood to reason one of the men would catch up with her at some point. She should have expected it, judging from the way they were shadowing her around the room. She just never expected it to be in the cloak closet.

Mrs. Finnerty had misplaced the claim check for her fur and come to Emily in a tizzy. Emily had reassured her not to worry, but to set the woman's mind at ease, she'd gone into the closet to find the fur and check the number on the tag.

The room was dark and muffled, but she knew, instantly, when someone else had entered. Her first thought came with a flare of excitement that perhaps it was Ash. Which was ridiculous, given everything that had happened between them. The last thing she should feel was this exhilarating lift of her spirits at the prospect he might have followed her.

The click of the door echoed through her bones. She whirled around and froze. Her heart sank. Her pulse pounded painfully in her temples. Because it wasn't Ash.

It was Roman.

And he was drunk.

"Emily," he burbled, stepping closer, caging her, blocking her in.

Horror howled. "Paula?" She called. Hopefully someone at the counter would hear. Hopefully someone saw him come in after her.

She scanned the small room, desperately hunting for a weapon. There was no guarantee Roman wouldn't try *that* again. He'd caught her alone at a frat party once in college. She'd not been feeling well and had gone to the ladies' room. When she emerged, he'd been waiting at the door. He'd snagged her around the waist and dragged her into a nearby bedroom. Forced her onto the bed. Thrown his heavy weight on top of her and…

She could taste her rising gorge at the memory.

It was not happening again.

It was not.

But it was. She could feel it humming on the air

With every step he took toward her, she took a step back until she hit the wall. He followed, pressed against her, his breath hot on her neck.

She hated feeling like this. Helpless.

"Paula? Jackson?" A panicked cry.

Nothing. No response.

"Don't bother," Roman rumbled, fumbling with her skirt. "There's no one there."

Something cold dribbled down her spine. It felt like panic. Her fingers curled around something—an umbrella? Hardly a weapon, but it wasn't all she had. Fury rose inside her too. Fury at what he'd done. The way he'd made her feel. How that one incident had flavored the whole of her life with fear.

Rage surged within her. Rage at all of them.

At Roman for trying to rape her when she'd been only seventeen, and trying to intimidate her again now. And Ash for using her and tossing her aside. But the worst of it she reserved for herself. For letting them treat her like she wasn't important. For allowing feelings for one of them to endure.

But Ash was the least of her worries now. Right now Roman, pressing against her, rubbing his erection against her, was the imminent threat.

Denial howled through her soul.

No. No. No.

Not again.

Not anymore.

She lifted the umbrella and brought in down on his foot. Hard.

He howled, lurched back. "What the fu—"

She brought up her weapon, jabbing the pointy end in his direction. Roman danced back to avoid it.

"You always were a bitch," he sneered, which was hardly fair. Every day of her life, she'd bent over backwards to be polite. Every day until now.

Something inside her snapped.

"Get out," she snarled.

"What?" She wasn't sure what surprised him the most, having a woman fight back or the fact that Emily Donahue was allowing herself to be rude. But she hardly cared. They were both things that needed to happen.

There was a time to be polite and there was a time to kick some ass.

"Get out or I'll skewer you."

Unbelievably, Roman laughed. "You'll skewer me with an umbrella?"

She jabbed him.

He yelped, which she found very satisfying, but then an angry look descended on his face. He grabbed the umbrella, yanked it from her grasp and tossed it aside. He glared at her, his intent simmering in hot waves.

She had the sudden sense she'd just poked a feral bear.

He lumbered toward her, blocking out the light. Terror clawed at her. She still had her knee, she reminded herself. And her thumbs. And she knew how to use them. She and Kaitlin had both taken self-defense classes after that disastrous party and now it was time to find out if they had been worth the money.

Apparently not. Apparently predators knew all the moves too. As she raised her hands, he captured her wrists. At the same time, he shoved his knees between hers and pressed her hard against the wall.

She hated his laugh. It rumbled through her like a claxon.

Her vision clouded. Her muscles seized. Her mind went numb.

It was happening again. It was—

The door opened, flooding the room with sound and light.

And yelling.

"What the fuck?"

Emily nearly fainted as Ash's outraged bellow rocked her. *Thank God*, she thought. *Thank God*.

He wrenched Roman around and stared at Emily. A muscle flexed in his cheek. "Are you okay?" he clipped. She understood what he was really asking. *Do you want this?*

"No."

"Okay." Before she could say anything more, before she could react or move or anything, his fist plowed into Roman's cheek and the bulkier man went reeling. Emily stepped aside and let him fall, insensate, onto the floor.

When Ash yanked her into his arms and held her, she let him. The comfort, the relief, was dizzying. He stroked her hair and murmured into her ear and she realized, she was crying. "Let it out," he said. "Just let it out."

"Ash," she gulped. "I need to get out of here." The room was closing in on her, making it hard to breathe.

"Of course."

He led her out into the hall and barked, "Get security in there," at Paula who was just returning with a plate of appetizers. Paula glanced into the cloak room, and rushed off to get help. But Ash didn't wait.

He quickly guided Emily down the hall and into a small lounge next to the ladies' room, sat on the sofa and settled her on his lap. And held her. "It's okay," he kept saying, though whether he was trying to convince her or himself, she wasn't sure. And she didn't care.

She wanted to stay here forever, in his arms.

This man with whom she'd had a one night stand.

The man who'd been her first.

Her only.

The man who had devastated her.

If she let him, he'd do it again.

She wanted to stay here forever, in his arms. But she couldn't.

So she stood and edged toward the other side of the room. The distance did not make her feel any safer. Because the real threat was in her heart.

"Thank you, Ash," she said, wiping her cheeks with the back of her hand. "Thank you for...saving me."

"I'm glad I listened my gut and followed Roman. He's an ass," he muttered.

She snorted a laugh, and then caught it halfway.

He met her gaze. Held it. "I'm an ass too."

"I beg your pardon?" Those were not the words she'd expected to hear.

He smiled. It wasn't a cocky, smarmy smile. It was threaded with humility and a hesitancy she'd never before seen in him.

"Emily."

"A-Ash."

"I was wondering if...we could talk."

She blinked. "T-talk? O-okay."

His lips parted, as though he wanted to say something but couldn't think of the words. And then, after a long, dangling pause, "God, you're beautiful."

Heat raced through her. Ribbons of elation. Her body softened.

She knew it was stupid. This was a guy who used women. Unrepentantly.

He'd used her.

Admitted it.

She was so many kinds of a fool for still wanting him. Aching for him.

But she did.

So when he took a step forward, she didn't back away, like a sane woman would. She held her ground. He stopped about a foot away.

While she appreciated that he gave her space, she yearned to feel his arms around her again, a clawing need. She reminded herself to remain aloof. To not fling herself into his embrace. She'd leaped into tempting waters with him before, and regretted it.

"I've missed you, Emily. More than I can say."

"You…missed me?" She choked on the words. She meant to say them in an incredulous tone, but she missed the mark. To her ears, they sounded feathery and breathy and befuddled. She shook her head. Rallied her resistance. Firmed her resolve.

Yes, he was gorgeous in that crisply pressed tux. Yes, his cologne drifted out and clogged her senses with a raging lust.

But he was Mr. One Night Stand. And she, apparently, was an easy mark.

She reminded herself of her vow—no more emotional decisions—and she took a step back. Something flickered over his expression. It might have been pain, but that was ludicrous. Guys like Ash Bristol didn't feel pain, remorse, regret. They just took what they wanted and then walked away.

Sorrow welled in her chest. She willed the tears prickling her lashes not to fall. She would not let him see her cry. She crossed her arms and attempted a smirk, although she wasn't good at smirking. She hadn't had much practice. "What do you want, Ash? Another roll in the hay? Because, according to your rules, our *convocation* has expired."

He winced. Raked his hair. "Emily…" He cleared his throat. "I just wanted to apologize. For what I did and said. I was wrong. That's all. I'm sorry. And for the record, I will always regret hurting you. Until the day I die." He shoved his hands into his pockets and gazed at her, as though memorizing her face. And then he turned. To leave.

To leave.

She thought she felt panic before? It was nothing compared to this rampant dread. If he walked out that door she knew, *knew*, she would never see him again.

"Ash!"

He froze. Waited.

But the words she wanted to say, ached to say—*stay, hold me, love me*—

would not come out. The part of her brain in charge of survival would not allow it. Instead, she folded her fingers together and offered the sweetest smile she could manage. "Thank you very much for saving me."

His eyes narrowed. As though he didn't like her formality, which was ridiculous. He was the one who had ended things between them. Or her demeanor, which was also ridiculous. She was only being civil.

"Quit being so damn polite."

She gaped at him. "I beg your pardon?"

"No." When she tipped her head to the side in confusion, he repeated himself. "No. You never beg my pardon. Never. In fact, I beg yours. I meant what I said Emily. I was an ass and I'm sorry."

She opened her mouth. Closed it again. Her brain fizzled and popped but she couldn't make any intelligible words come out. Finally, at long last, she managed, "That's okay, Ash."

"No, damn it. It's not. It's not okay." His vehemence surprised her. "I've been hurt in relationships, Emily. And I liked you. I liked you so much I was scared of getting hurt again. So instead…" he fixed her with a remorseful look. "Instead I hurt you. And I'm sorry. Can you forgive me?"

Excitement, hope and annoyance swirled inside her. She wasn't sure which to focus on. She settled for politeness. "I… Of course Ash. I understand."

He glared at her.

She didn't know why he glared at her. She was accepting his apology after all. "What?" she asked.

"Would it make you feel better to hit me?"

"What?"

"Because it would make me feel better if you hit me. Yelled at me. Punished me. Something."

For some reason, his outburst made her unaccountably happy. She laughed. "I'm not going to hit you. And I'm not going to yell."

He grimaced. "Punishment then?"

She folded her hands before her and then deliberately unfolded them. "That depends."

"On what?"

"On where we go from here."

She liked the way his gaze warmed. "So… You are willing to…give me another chance? Would you…" He ran his finger around his collar. "Would you…go out on a date with me?"

Her heart faltered. "I don't think that would be wise." Not just yet, anyway. "But we can be friends."

He swallowed. "Friends?"

She nibbled her lower lip. "I…would like to get to know you better."

"I'd like to get to know you better. I really would." The way he said it, the glint in his eye made her knees weak.

She ignored it. The glint. The wobbly knees. The thudding pulse. She stepped toward him and thrust out a hand. "Friends?"

His Adam's apple worked as he stared at her offering. Then he slid his hand into hers. As their palms kissed, electricity sizzled through her. She stepped closer.

As did he.

Until they were face to face, chest to chest, breath to breath—

"Emily!"

They sprang apart. Emily whirled to see Kaitlin in the doorway.

Kaitlin's gaze flicked from her to Ash and back again. Narrowed. "Are you…okay?"

Emily laughed. She didn't know why she laughed, other than the joy filling her heart. And Kaitlin's expression. "Yes. I'm okay."

"And the two of you? Did you work it out?"

Emily and Ash exchanged a glance. His brow lifted, as though in question.

"For now," she said. "We've made peace."

He nodded. "We're friends." Though the way he said the word, he didn't sound thrilled.

"Oh Thank God," Kaitlin gusted. "Because I have something to tell you." She flicked a guilt-ridden look at Ash.

"What is it?"

"Well, I kept Roman from winning your auction item, but the bidding closed before I realized…"

"Realized what?"

"The high bidder was…Ash."

Emily whirled on him. "You bid on my item?"

He shrugged. "I didn't want Roman to get it. So I won?" He tried to wipe his smile away, but Emily caught it.

"You won."

"Hours and hours with Emily?"

Kaitlin chuckled. "Mmm hmm. I warn you, she's a slave driver when it comes to these charity events."

The wink he shot Emily was a trifle wicked. "Ah," he murmured. "Punishment it is."

CHAPTER TWELVE

Ash was not a man to let grass grow under his feet. Especially when it came to an opportunity to spend time with Emily. Using the event she had pledged to help him with as an excuse, he invited her out the next day to talk about the details over coffee.

He would have preferred taking her to his penthouse for something more intimate, but he was determined to take this wooing slowly. Her words had made it clear she had only friendship in mind, but her eyes told a different story. He suspected her feelings ran as deeply for him as his did for her, but he had to take his time.

He'd hurt her, and until he made it up to her, until he won back her trust, friendship would have to do.

Friendship was probably best. No physical contact. Or at least, very little. Kissing, perhaps. And he knew if he had her alone in his apartment, more would happen than kissing. A lot more.

There was something about her he just found irresistible. He wasn't sure if it was her bright, shining innocent outlook on life, or her smile or just her scent, but when he was around her, he seemed to lose all sanity. He wanted nothing more than to pull her into his arms and make passionate love to her.

So coffee it was.

They met at Beanie's Book and Coffee in Montlake, which was awkward, because the shop was owned by Emily's friends, Lucy and Kristi. Who had, apparently, been clued in about his bad behavior. So as Ash and Emily chatted, they hovered and glared. After a while, Bella and Holt showed up to hover and glare as well. As though Lucy had called for reinforcements.

Ash ignored them. They could hover and glare all they wanted. As long as he was with Emily, he didn't care. Every moment together was a chance to show her the kind of man he really was. Or at least the kind of man he was trying to be. Every moment together was a chance to win her back.

"So have you decided on a charity?" she asked as she sipped her mocha. He loved the pouf of whipped cream clinging to her nose. He wanted to lap it off, but knew better. Holt liked to flex his muscles when he hovered.

"I have." After five minutes thought, he'd settled on a cause for his big fund-raiser and as soon as the idea lit in his brain, he knew it was something he needed to do.

"What is it?" She leaned forward. He tried not to peep at the cleavage the movement exposed and failed.

"I…ah…" His brain fizzled as she leaned forward even more. Hell, if he didn't know any better, he'd suspect she was trying to torment him. Then again, he had given her carte blanche to punish him. But only because he knew she'd never take him up on it. Not his Emily…

"Ash?"

"Huh? What?" He blinked.

"Your charity?"

"Oh. Right." He pulled out the folder he'd brought. "It's a great organization that finds mentors for foster kids."

She flipped through the prospectus. "Fostering the Future? I've heard of them. But…"

"But what?"

She fixed those beautiful blue eyes on him. They sliced right through to his soul. "Why does it matter to you?" When he didn't answer, her chin firmed. "It has to matter, Ash. These events are a lot of work and if you don't have a passion for it, it won't be a success."

"I do. Have a passion…"

She crossed her arms. "Why?"

"I, ah, well…" Again, her attention dislodged all logical thought. He sucked in a breath and pulled the folder back, focusing on that instead. "Okay. When I was ten my mom had just gone through her fifth divorce."

She made a little sympathy coo, but he ignored it. There was no need for sympathy anymore. He was over all of that.

"And my dad was between wives—" Another coo. He shot a look at her, trying not to frown. "Okay, the Bristols aren't known for marital longevity. Not something I'm proud of."

To his surprise, she put her hand on his. "Ash. It's not your fault your parents didn't stay married."

"I didn't stay married very long either."

"Would-would you like to tell me why?" This, she asked softly.

His pulse thudded in the silence. He knew if he was ever going to have anything with her, she needed to know. Deserved to know. But damn, the words were hard to say. "She didn't love *me*. She married me for my money." There. Bold. Brash. Raw.

He did not expect her reaction. A combination of fury and outrage. For him. "What a bitch." The use of that invective from Emily's lips shocked him. It warmed him too.

"It gets worse." He raked his fingers through his hair. "She made this announcement on our honeymoon..."

"No."

"She'd been angling for my father, but he'd just met Michelle. So she switched to me. All she wanted was a settlement." He was mortified at the way the sentence ended, all wretched and forlorn. He hadn't intended it that way. But even now, his heart shrank when he thought of it.

"Oh, Ash. I'm so sorry." Emily stared down at her coffee. "I can't think of a better reason to end a marriage."

"It was a bad breakup. In a series of bad breakups. That's why... That's why I decided on a rule. One night stands only." He fiddled with his spoon. "I just came to the conclusion that a real relationship wasn't in the cards for me." A flush crawled up his cheeks. "As though I was cursed or something."

Her mouth opened. Closed. She swallowed. "I see."

"I know it sounds stupid when I say the words out loud. But that's how I felt. Can you understand that?"

"I can." Her tone was thick with emotion. "I've felt the same way."

Her hand still rested on his. He turned his palm up, so they were holding hands, and stroked her with his thumb. "I can't imagine that." She was too perfect. Too sweet to feel as though the world was against her.

"Every experience I've had with a man has been...well, terrible."

He winced. Yeah. He probably deserved that.

"All I ever wanted was to find *him*."

"Him?" He tightened his hold on her.

"You know." She laughed self-consciously. "Prince Charming. Instead I found Prince Ogre. And Prince Toad..."

"And Prince Ass," he couldn't help but add.

She chuckled. "You weren't so bad."

"Thank you?"

"Until you dumped me..."

He winced.

"I just haven't had much luck." She sighed. "Of course, when I was in high school, boys never approached me. They were scared of my dad."

"Your dad?"

She waggled her brows. "He's scary."

Ash laughed.

"Needless to say, I didn't date. And then, in college...there was an unpleasant incident."

Shit. The way she said it made prickles crawl up his spine. He didn't want to ask, but had to. "What-what kind of incident?"

Her lashes veiled her eyes. She drew circles on the table with a fingertip. "A…something similar to what happened last night."

Hackles rose. "How similar?"

Her expression lanced him. "Exactly similar."

"Roman?"

She nodded.

Rage swept through him like a forest fire. *I will kill him*, he thought. *I will fucking kill him*. But he didn't say it. Couldn't speak.

"Anyway, I started thinking *I* was cursed."

Ash swallowed the lump in his throat. "You're not cursed."

"That some malicious fairy had dumped a load of ug-dust on my head as a baby."

"You're not cursed. And what is ug-dust?"

"The opposite of pretty-dust."

He gaped at her. She was beautiful. The most beautiful creature on the planet. How could she think she was anything but magnificent?

"Em—"

"Hey there." Lucy chirped, stepping up to their table with a plastic smile on her lips. Lucy was a drop-dead gorgeous platinum blonde, but her eyes spat daggers. At Ash. "How's it going? All finished?" She scooped up Ash's cup, though it was half full.

Emily frowned. "We're not done Lucy. Shoo."

Lucy leaned in. "'Kay. But just a heads up. Holt's getting twitchy."

Ash glanced over his shoulder just in time to see the behemoth at the coffee bar crack his knuckles.

"Tell him to take a chill pill," Emily said, waggling her fingers toward Holt with a devil-may-care insouciance. Then again, she wasn't the one Holt was gunning for.

"I will. But…" Lucy frowned at their entwined hands. "You might want to keep it on your side of the table, Bristol." With that, she whirled and flounced away.

Emily made a face. "Sorry about that."

"I love that they're so protective of you."

She wrinkled her nose. "I'm not a baby."

"No. But you are trusting and sweet. You see the best in people and expect them to act on it…"

"I don't see the best in people. Ash," she corrected. "I look for it. There's a difference. Now, before you get too distracted, you were telling me why this charity matters to you."

"Right."

"Your parents had both just divorced…"

"My mom had just divorced. My dad was between wives."

"There's a difference?"

"There is."

"I see. And?"

"And I was having a hard time with it. Okay. Let's be honest. I was being a total shit. To everyone. Then one day, my dad brought home this skinny kid. Said he was in foster care. Said we were going to "mentor" him. I thought my dad had gone around the bend. What I didn't realize was, he had done this for me. I needed a reminder."

"A reminder?"

"Of how good I had it. Even though my life wasn't perfect, at least I had someone. This kid had no one. Nothing."

"He had no one?"

"No one. His parents were dead and he had no relatives. He was shuttled from foster home to foster home, school to school. And…there were other issues too. Anyway, my dad took him under his wing. Practically made him a part of the family. We went to baseball games and on fishing trips and out to the island. Every time I turned around, there he was.

"At first I resented the hell out of him. He was nothing but a mopey pain in the ass, but as I got to know him I realized, he was a great guy. And he'd been through…well, he'd been through hell." Ash fiddled with the corner of the folder. While he wanted to tell Emily all the details, it wasn't his story to share. "At any rate, my dad was his mentor all through his teen years…he even lived with us for a while when he aged out of foster care. We made damn sure he went to college." He fixed his gaze on the file and lowered his voice. "He ended up being the best friend I've ever had. It horrifies me to think what would have happened to him if my dad hadn't stepped in. I suspect the reason Parker is alive today is because of this program. I know his success is a direct result of Fostering the Future."

"Parker?"

Shit. He hadn't meant to say his name. "He's like a brother to me."

"All right then." Emily sat back. "Fostering the Future it is. So Ash, what do you want to accomplish with this fund-raiser?"

"Accomplish?"

"What are your goals? How much money do you want to raise? That determines the kind of venue, the people we invite, you know. Stuff like that."

"Ah. Yeah." Money. Money meant nothing. If he'd learned anything in life it was that money could not solve every problem. He leaned forward, ignoring the bristling giant at the coffee bar. "What I'd really like to do, I mean, what they really need, are more mentors. Businessmen and women who want to give their time and knowledge to help a kid get back on his feet. Or her feet…"

"There are girls in the program too?"

"Yes. It's about half and half right now."

"And how many clients do they currently have…"

Emily went on to ask questions and Ash answered when necessary, but his attention was riveted on her. On her face, the way it lit up and shone, the animation of her features when an idea came to her. She madly scribbled notes as they talked.

She threw out names of potential donors who would also be excellent mentors; it seemed like she knew everyone who was anyone in Seattle society.

God, she was incredible.

It occurred to him that she would make a perfect wife for a man in his position. Especially if he took over more responsibilities at the foundation. After the disaster of his marriage, he'd decided if he ever married, he'd probably need to choose someone from his own financial strata, just to avoid the risk of marrying a gold digger.

Now he saw that idea for the idiocy it was.

Emily was perfect for him.

Even without being rich.

She would love him for himself…if she ever did fall in love with him. She would be faithful and warm and make him laugh. They would be a perfect match.

They *were* a perfect match.

All he had to do was convince *her* of that.

He was suddenly more determined than ever to make that happen. He glanced over his shoulder. But it wouldn't happen here. Not with chaperones in tow.

"Okay," she gusted, recapturing his attention. Or part of it. "Here's what I'm thinking."

"Yes?"

"Because we want to find mentors for these kids, it's crucial to get the kids and the potential mentors together. So they can interact. The thought is, once they meet these kids and see how great they are, they won't be able to resist."

"Um. Okay." Sounded good.

She winked. "It works with homeless kittens too. Anyway, what do you say about this… We hold a weekend party on the island. We have the donors come down on Friday for a swanky soiree, you know, to soften them up. And then bring in the kids on Saturday for a beach luau. We'll have games and activities so they can all get to know each other." She tapped her lips. "Maybe fireworks? And then on Sunday we'll hit them with the call to mentor, and hit them hard. I know it's a tight clock, but I'd like to have the event before school starts. That would give us a little less than a month. Two weeks at the soonest." Her eyes shone. "What do you think, Ash?"

What did he think?

She was perfect.

Absolutely perfect.

And he was going to win her.

No. Matter. What.

Excitement danced through Emily as she reviewed the details of the event. She loved this kind of project. Especially one with such potential impact.

But there was more to it than that. It was this. Spending time with Ash. Working with him on a project that meant something.

Already, in this short period of time, she'd learned so much about him. About what made him tick.

She had been attracted to him on a physical level the instant she'd set eyes on him. Now, she saw through to his soul. The Ash behind the mask he presented to the world.

She could see the ten-year-old boy, lost and confused when the foundation of his life had crumbled. She could see the wounded man, deeply in love and cut to the core by his bride's betrayal.

She could understand why he vowed to keep his distance from pain, why he swore never to be hurt like that again.

She, after all, had sworn the same thing. And it had ruled her life for far too long.

She would not allow it to rule her anymore.

Yes, she could see the depth of Ash Bristol's soul. And she liked it.

She liked him.

She wanted…more.

As incomprehensible as it was, after everything that had happened between them, she wanted more. She was willing, ready, to try again.

Emily glanced at her friends, pretending not to ogle them. Then she smiled at Ash. "I think we're done here."

His face fell. "Already?"

"Yep. There's lots more to do, but I think we have the bones down."

"Already?" Was it her imagination, or did he not want to end their tête-à-tête?

She put a palm on her stomach. "I'm hungry. How about you?"

He perked up at that. "Yeah."

"What do you say we get out of here and go somewhere…more private?"

He really perked up at that. "Is this a…date?"

"Maybe." Her lips twitched.

He beamed at her. And then he sobered and cleared his throat. "I should probably warn you, Holt's not going to like us dating. Lane either." Then, after a moment of reflection, "And probably Drew."

"True." Emily nibbled her inner cheek. "So it's probably best if we don't take them on any of our dates."

"Agreed." Humor laced his tone. "But how do we lose them?"

"Easy. We shake hands, and then you gather your things and leave."

"Leave?"

"I'll pretend I'm going to the restroom and sneak out the back door. We can meet in the parking lot. You did bring your car?"

He nodded.

"Perfect. We can escape and go have dinner somewhere."

"Where would you like to go?"

She shrugged. "Anywhere." Anywhere with him.

His eyes lit. "I know just the place. There's…something special I'd like to show you."

"Okay." She thrust out her hand. He took it. And though the handshake was utterly decorous, it gave Emily an unholy thrill.

Because she and Ash were going on a secret date.

CHAPTER THIRTEEN

He took her out for teriyaki, which was not what she'd been expecting. When he'd said, *I want to show you something special,* she'd thought, at the very least, it would involve linen tablecloths. But she was a fan of teriyaki, and this was some of the best she'd ever had. And they were together.

And Holt wasn't hovering.

All in all, it was pretty awesome.

When they were full, they pushed their plates and chopsticks to the side and Ash leaned forward. "Emily, can we talk?"

She nibbled her lip. "We are talking." They'd been talking all evening. Just not about anything real.

"You know what I mean."

"Oookay." Her belly flipped, making her wish she hadn't eaten that second egg roll.

"What are we going to do about this thing?"

Emily blinked. "This thing?"

"This thing between us?"

Oh. That thing.

She fiddled with the paper from her straw. Rolled it into a ball. "I dunno."

He took her hand, quieting her restlessness. When she looked up, he snagged her gaze. The heat of his intent burned her. "Please tell me there's a chance for us. A real chance."

Heavens, he was attractive. Even with his muscles tight, his expression stark, his cheeks flushed. Everything about him radiated sincerity.

She couldn't help but be impressed. He didn't strike her as a man who begged often. If ever.

She wanted to give him another chance. She really did. But—

"I'll be honest, Ash. I'm afraid."

He winced. "Of me?"

A little nod. "Of getting hurt again."

"I won't hurt you. Ever again. I swear." When she didn't respond, he blew out a harsh breath. "Okay. I understand—"

She silenced him with a finger to his lips. He froze at her touch. Closed his eyes and sighed.

"I don't think you do, Ash. I like you. I do. More than I should, I suppose. More than my friends think I should…"

He grimaced.

"I should just walk away…but I can't. I feel like there's something…something here."

"With us?"

"Yes. With us."

His tension broke; a smile wreathed his face, making him more handsome than ever. "Thank God."

"But Ash, you do realize it's going to take time for me to—"

"Yes. I realize that. I'm prepared to wait. For as long as it takes."

She frowned. "It could take a while."

"I understand. Though…if you've decided on my punishment, that might speed things up."

Emily blinked. "Your what?"

"Remember? We agreed. You should punish me for being an ass. You should think of something."

"I should?"

"It would make me feel better."

"Even the playing field?"

"Something like that." He sat back. "Is it selfish of me to want to clear the slate?"

She shook her head. Tried not to grin. "Maybe I should just use you."

"What?"

"You know. Use your body."

He gaped at her.

"Maybe I should use you and toss you aside…"

His throat worked. "I-I couldn't blame you if you did."

Silly boy.

Little did he know, she was only teasing. She couldn't toss him aside if her life depended on it. "Let's just take it one day at a time. Okay?"

He nodded. "Okay."

It seemed as though that was enough for him. For now. He sat back in his chair and exhaled what might have been a breath of relief.

"Was there something you wanted to show me?"

"Oh. Yeah." His features lit up. He tossed some bills on the table and grabbed her hand, towing her after him out the door and down the street to a small building a block from the restaurant.

"What is it?" she asked as he pulled out a key and unlocked the door.

"My shop."

"Your...shop?" But when he opened the door and ushered her in with a flourish, she understood. The smell of solder and baby powder was unmistakable to someone familiar with glass art. "Oh my goodness." She glanced around. It was a small space, brightly lit once he flicked on the fluorescent overheads and, heavens, the workshop was a treasure trove.

She flitted from one bench to another, oohing and aahing like a child at Christmas, checking out his array of tools and molds and soldering irons, the stands of uncut glass, in a myriad of colors. "This is incredible."

"These are my kilns," he said, showing her several, lined up against the wall, different sizes ranging from the largest they made to a small one perfect for bead and jewelry making. "Would you like to see my most recent projects?"

She nodded. "Please."

He headed for a shelf on the far side of the room and pulled a towel off a long, elegant glass platter.

Emily stilled. For there, playing out in the ethereal lines of glass, was a scene burned into her memory. It was the island, their island, in a sapphire swirling sea with the backdrop of a glorious sunset, burnt umber streaked with yellow and red. "Oh—" Her voice caught. "Ash. It's beautiful. How...how did you do this?"

"It was easy. I started with a photograph of the island, and then cut out the forms. The island, the water and the sky. I fit them together and fused them on a base. Then I slumped the platter on the tray form."

She stared at him. He made it sound so simple. Having done fused art, she knew it hadn't been. Just cutting the glass so there were no gaps would have taken her hours. The fusing phase could take a full day in the kiln depending on the temperature. And annealing was an art in itself. "I love it. It's our island, isn't it?"

He nodded.

"What's this speck?" She peered at an odd black spot on the ripple glass of the water.

He cleared his throat. "That's a couple on a Jet Ski."

She bent down for a better look. Astoundingly, it was. Tiny, as though he'd painted it with a thread, but without a doubt, the form of tiny couple jetting across the water for an island tryst.

"I couldn't stop thinking of you."

"It's lovely, Ash. Just lovely."

"I made this one too." He removed the cover on another platter, featuring the image of an exquisite eagle in flight. "And this one..." A tiny cabin perched on a cliff over crashing waves. "And this one..." A silhouette. Two people a breath away from a kiss.

The lines were exquisite. Haunting. Devastating.

Only those who created art understood. It wasn't just a pretty piece of glass lying there. It was a chunk of his soul. Need and pain etched in every line.

She set her palm to his cheek. "I love them."

"I made them for you."

Her heart fluttered. He'd spent so much time on these exquisite pieces. And all the while, thinking of her. It was a thrilling thought. Heady. Humbling. There was no doubt in her mind, he meant every word he said. "You are-you are very talented, Ash."

"Thank you." He kissed her palm, but didn't move closer, though he could have, if he'd wanted to. Right now, she would have allowed him almost anything.

She tried not to be annoyed that he didn't take advantage of her vulnerability. To hide her feelings, she pretended to study his workshop. "Do you come here often?"

He took her cue and stepped away. "I, ah, not as often as I'd like. I'd like to have a studio at home." He chuckled. "But I can't get zoned for the kilns. So I come here, sometimes for days at a time, and work. When I get hungry, I eat teriyaki."

"And when you get tired?"

"There's a bed in the ba—"

He broke off, as though he'd just realized what he'd said. Or just *remembered* there was a bed in the back. With a suddenness that stunned her, the energy around them shifted.

The muscles in his face went tight. Something ticked in his cheek. The moment hung for an endless eternity. Tension throbbed between them.

Was that all it took? She wondered with a self-directed snort. The mention of a bed in the vicinity?

Apparently.

Because, as one, they moved. Toward each other. In a rush.

They met in the middle of the room, chest to chest, groin to groin. He wrapped his strong arms around her and she curled around him. He didn't kiss her. They kissed each other. A wild scalding, heart-pounding manic exchange that left her light-headed and elated.

There was no apathy in the kiss. No politeness. No civility. It was savage. Savage need. Savage hunger. Savage delight.

His lips raked hers. His tongue thrust in. He consumed her. She responded in kind, unable, unwilling, to draw back.

This. This. This was what she wanted. What she needed. What she craved.

His essence, his taste, his scent, infused her, maddened her, aroused her.

"Ash," she whispered. "Ash."

"Emily." He nested in the crook of her neck, sucking, ravaging, enervating, every nerve.

His hand stroked down her arm, up her ribs and—she sucked in a breath, and yes—he cupped her breast. Thumbed a nipple. Sensation rained through her, scored her, scorched her. She gave a feral cry. His hold tightened, his intensity flared. "God, Emily."

The material of her skirt danced over her thighs as he bunched it up. She knew she should stop him. But she couldn't stop him. Her body ached, hungered, sang.

When he scraped her tender center, she seized. Excitement lanced her. He pressed against that swollen, aching nub, making wide circles, and then smaller ones, narrowing in, centering all her attention on that one smoldering spot.

She gasped as pleasure lanced her, and then gasped again when he slipped beneath the band of her panties and touched her.

"Oh, Em," he growled.

She knew she was wet. Drenched. Weeping for him.

He delved deeper between her folds. She spread her legs a bit to allow him entrance. Because, God, she wanted this. Needed this. And, oh…

He eased in. Two thick, long fingers.

Shudders wracked her. Agony and joy and hunger assailed her. A sound, like a hiss, escaped through her teeth.

He explored, ruthless, determined, seeking and finding that spot that made her clench, rail, fist his hair and howl. He covered her mouth, muffling her wail, drinking it in, driving her higher and higher. His tongue mimicked his thrusts below.

Changing his angle, he drove deep, massaging her inside, and obliterating her senses with a wicked scrape of his thumb over her thrumming clit.

She seized. Exploded. Came.

Rapture stole her breath. Ecstasy, perfect and absolute. She dissolved. Dissolved into the pleasure like a sugar castle in the rain.

After her crisis, she expected him to take her. To unfasten his jeans and shove into her like a stallion. Take what he'd earned. Take it and walk away.

But he didn't. He held her, soothed her…and then let the hem of her skirt fall.

She lifted her head and stared into his eyes. She loved those eyes. Loved even more that they were warm when he looked at her, rather than cold, as they'd been that day on the beach.

Still, he set her aside. Gently.

"Aren't we going to… You know?"

He stood and crossed the room, though she could tell it cost him.

"We're not doing that," he said. "Not until we know each other better. Remember?"

She put out a lip. She'd like to. She'd like to right now.

"We need to take it slow."

"Slow?" She wasn't sure how she felt about that. After what had just happened, after his heart-felt apology, after seeing his art, after that scorching…whatever it had been. Now she just wanted more. But she sensed he needed time. Needed the chance to feel redeemed.

"I'll be on my best behavior."

"No more kissing?"

A flush tinged his cheeks. He chewed on his inner cheek as he thought that over. "Well, maybe kissing. But that's it. Until we know each other better."

She nodded. "That sounds fair."

She could live with that. After all, every kiss they'd shared had led to something more. And quickly.

Surely getting to know each other wouldn't take too long…

Every day for the next week they worked on the fund-raiser and every evening, Ash took Emily out. They went to dinner, saw a couple of shows, and even went on a whale-watching cruise on Saturday. He loved witnessing her reactions to that, especially when an Orca surfaced and then breeched right next to their boat. He loved how she found joy in the simplest things. The sparkle of sunlight on the water, the feel of the spray, the clasp of his hand.

They talked and laughed and discovered they had a lot in common, which surprised him. It did not surprise him that they were such a good fit together. Sometimes, all they had to do was exchange a glance to know what the other was thinking.

She loved fishing and camping and, holy God, football.

She was, very probably, a perfect woman.

This relationship was unlike any other he'd had. It scared him a bit, but thrilled him too. Realization, recognition thrummed through him. The certainty that she was the one for him.

After each date he took her home and kissed her goodnight on her porch. Just kissed her. He lived for those kisses. It took everything in him to resist the temptation to succumb to her invitation to come in. But he was determined. And stubborn.

And, perhaps, a little stupid.

On Sunday, they went to the Pike Place Market and enjoyed a day of grazing and people watching. She adored the tiny donuts and the flying fish and tasting cheese that had been made before their eyes.

He adored being with her.

They returned to her house that afternoon full to the brim with delicious food, arms laden with packages and the flowers he'd bought her, just because she'd admired them.

He stopped before her door, as he always did, though she opened it and looked at him expectantly.

"Are you coming in?"

Heat crawled up his neck. Hell. He wanted to. He really wanted to. But he wouldn't. He shook his head. "I shouldn't."

Her lip came out.

"I'll come back tomorrow night. Take you out for dinner." He kissed her on the forehead. The cheek. And then, because he couldn't resist, the tip of her nose.

Emily stepped closer. Tipped up her face. Stared into his eyes.

Damn, he could drown in that ocean.

He didn't know how much longer he could take this.

But he had to. He had to show her he was an honorable man.

Words simply weren't enough.

And this was far too important.

One kiss. That was all he would allow himself.

One kiss only.

His lips were gentle as they brushed hers, tender and sweet. Emily shuddered as arousal washed through her. When she opened her mouth, he pulled her closer, his hold firmed, he deepened the kiss.

She shifted her packages and, with her free hand, held him there, in place, as she tasted him. Shivers of delight skittered along her nerves.

But while she felt it, he, apparently didn't. Or he possessed the self-control to stop. Which annoyed her.

Lots of things annoyed her at that moment.

Most especially that he possessed the self-control to stop. To end the kiss and turn away with a casual, "I'll see you tomorrow," leaving her quivering there on the stoop.

She wanted to be wanted.

Insanely.

Uncontrollably.

Passionately.

She didn't doubt he wanted her. He did. It was clear in every line of his body as he walked back to his car. But he didn't want her enough. Enough to break through that annoying wall of reserve he had constructed.

And she found she wanted him to. Needed him to. Badly.

As Emily watched Ash drive away, a new determination flooded her. If he was a stubborn as he claimed, it might be a good idea to call in reinforcements.

CHAPTER FOURTEEN

"Thank you all so much for coming," Emily said as she picked up Prince Phillip and gently set him on the floor. She brushed off the cushion and sat. The Yorkie mix looked back at her with wounded eyes.

"Thanks for the invitation," Avery said, curling her long blonde hair around a shell-like ear. "It's been far too long since we've all gotten together."

"Why has it been so long?" Mel asked. She and Avery sat together on the floor playing with Beast and Li Shang, two of Emily's foster dogs, while Kaitlin, Jamie and Tara entertained the kittens on the couch. Bella sat in the other armchair, hugging a fuzzy pink pillow and glaring at the animals.

Avery sighed. "We've been busy, darling."

Mel smirked.

"How did that dungeon crawl go?" Bella asked. The curiosity in her tone surprised Emily because of all her friends, Bella was the last one she would expect to have an interest in the BDSM community.

Then again, she *was* dating Holt.

"It was awesomeballs," Mel said, lacing her fingers with Avery's. They shared a loverly glance that went on waaay too long.

Tara cleared her throat. "Much better than regular balls."

Avery chuckled. "Darling, anything is better than regular balls."

Naveen jumped on Jamie's lap and she "oofed." She resettled the Springer Spaniel so he wasn't goring her. "Emily, I've never known anyone who had so many animals."

"I think they're sweet," Kaitlin, already covered with cat fur, purred.

"They're *everywhere*." Bella shuddered, and then took a gulp of her wine. Bella was not an animal lover. But she did love wine. "Are you turning into a cat lady?"

Kaitlin laughed. "You know Emily. She can't resist a creature in need."

"The kittens are up for adoption," Emily suggested hopefully. Yes, she was a pushover for sweet furry faces, especially when they were slated for termination. Everyone at the shelter knew it. They made a point to walk her down "death row" whenever she visited. She almost always brought someone home. It was getting out of hand.

Clearly she needed a bigger house.

Perhaps something in the country.

Kaitlin grimaced. "You are evil, aren't you?" Kaitlin was also a sucker for tiny bundles of fur.

The kittens needed a good home.

And Kaitlin probably needed kittens.

In fact, all of her friends needed pets. Except for Bella who had scrunched herself into a ball in the armchair trying to avoid Aladdin's diligent kisses.

Kaitlin lowered her lashes and fixated on Brier Rose. They bumped noses and the kitten rubbed her cheek on Kaitlin's, marking her territory. Her human. Emily bit back a grin. Excellent. One down.

But she had reasons for inviting her friends over other than thinning her herd.

"So I suppose you are all wondering why I asked you here."

Kaitlin snorted. Emily should have known *she'd* figured it out.

"What?" Jamie asked, stroking the scruff on Naveen's neck.

"I've been seeing someone."

Bella wrinkled her nose. "Don't tell me it's *him*."

"Him who?" Beast nudged her hand and Avery pulled the three-legged puppy onto her lap and scratched him behind the ears until he grunted in bliss. Beast was an attention whore and loved a good scratch. Emily should probably warn Avery that he drooled, but decided to let her figure that out for herself.

"Ash the Ass," Bella grumbled.

"Wait. Ash? As in Ash Bristol?" Avery gasped.

Emily nodded.

"I can't believe, after everything he did, you're giving him another chance."

"Bella, hush," Kaitlin said.

Avery lifted a perfectly sculpted brow. "What did he do?"

"He lured Emily into a one night stand."

"Sounds like Ash."

"He didn't lure me anywhere." Emily jumped to her feet. "Are you going to listen or not? I need your help."

"With the fund-raiser?" Jamie asked.

Avery shot an apprehensive look at Emily. "What fund-raiser? Why didn't someone warn me there was a fund-raiser?"

Kaitlin smiled. "Emily and Ash are doing a fund-raiser for Fostering the Future together."

Avery blinked. "Ash Bristol."

"Yes."

"Doing a fund-raiser?"

"Of course."

"No of course about it, Boo. Of all the people in the world to be doing a fund-raiser, Ash Bristol would be the last name on my list. In fact, he wouldn't be on my list at all."

"I know," Bella muttered. "He's an ass."

Emily frowned at them both. "He's changed."

"He won Emily's help in a silent auction and picked Fostering the Future as his charity. I, for one, think that's wonderful." Bless Kaitlin's heart. She was everybody's champion.

"We should all help with the fund-raiser. Don't you agree?" Jamie said.

"I didn't ask you here for your help with the fund-raiser..." Emily paused and added, "Although I fully expect you all to help."

Avery issued a melodramatic, long-suffering sigh. "Naturally. How much do you need?"

"Well..."

"Oh God." Avery paled. "I know that look."

"I'm not asking for a donation, Ave."

Avery and Mel exchanged a glance. "Then what do you want?"

"Your house."

Avery's eyes bulged. "My house?"

"We're inviting the donors to the island for a weekend party. Now, Ash's house sleeps ten, Lane and Lucy's about the same. But your house..." She trailed off.

"You want me to open a B&B for charity?"

"Just for the weekend."

"'Scuse me." Mel leaned forward. "Like, the whole weekend?"

Emily nodded. "There will be about twenty couples and fifteen children."

"Oh, the children aren't staying at my place." Avery sliced her hand through the air to make the point. "No way."

Mel nodded. "That would not be wise."

"The kids can stay at our places. Boys at Ash's and girls with us. Sleeping bags in the basement. We need your place for the donors. And you," she whirled on Mel, "have to be on your best behavior."

"Does that mean I can't put Avery into a slave collar?" Mel grinned wickedly.

Emily pursed her lips. "It's not that kind of party."

Avery pouted. "I suppose that means we have to lock up the dungeon."

Though she blushed, Emily nodded primly. "That would be best."

Avery winked. "Wouldn't want one of your fancy donors wandering down there by accident."

"In my experience," Mel said, "there are no such accidents."

"Yes, please. Do lock up your dungeon."

"And put away all our pretty toys?"

"All of them?" Mel squealed, but Emily suspected she was teasing. "Oh, this will be like an Easter Egg Hunt."

Avery snorted a laugh. "Don't forget the ones in the freezer…"

"Could you imagine? Muffy goes in for a piece of ice and pulls out a butt pl—"

"Hookay," Emily gusted. "That would be awesome, Avery. Thank you Mel."

Mel winked. "My pleasure, princess."

"So wait, Ems." Kaitlin said. "If you didn't ask us here to help with your fund-raiser—"

"She asked us here to help with the fund-raiser," Avery corrected, but Kaitlin ignored her.

"Why did you invite us?"

Emily blushed. "I asked you here for your advice about Ash."

Bella tossed back her drink. "He's an ass."

"He did save her from Roman," Kaitlin reminded the assemblage.

"He did," Emily said, trying not to shudder at the memory of being cornered by that toad again.

Tara chuckled. "I heard Ash punched him right in the kisser."

"Black eye for a month," Jamie said in a pleasant tone.

Avery swirled her wine. "Serves Roman right. That creep should know better than to mess with our kind."

Everyone peeped at Avery. They all knew what she liked to do for fun. It usually involved handcuffs and whips. Maybe peanut butter.

Tara sat back as Li Shang, Emily's foster Chow, crawled onto her lap. "You would be an awesome Avenger, Aves."

Avery chuckled. "Don't I know it."

Kaitlin jumped as Ariel crawled up her skirt to nestle in her lap as kittens do—claws first. When she scratched the ball of fur behind the ears, Jasmine and Snow joined their sister on a friendly lap. They'd all learned not to bother Bella. "So Emily, what's the problem with Ash?"

"He's Ash?" Bella offered.

Kaitlin ignored her. "Are you still attracted to him?"

"Oh, yes."

"But he's an ass." This—surprise, surprise—from Bella.

"And you think he has potential?"

"Even though he's an ass?"

They both ignored Bella.

"Well? Do you?"

"Yes." Emily took a sip of her water. It was uncomfortable being the center of all this attention, even though all these girls were her friends. "From the moment I saw him I knew... I thought...perhaps...he might be... I dunno." She flushed.

"What?" Bella snapped. "Your Knight in Shining Armor?" She narrowed her eyes at Emily's expression. "No. You've gotta be shitting me."

"He has unplumbed depths," Kaitlin insisted, and a flood of gratitude rose in Emily's breast. God bless Kaitlin.

"He does. I mean, he has walls..."

"Who doesn't?"

"Right? But I see something in him. Something worth knowing. Something special."

Everyone around the room nodded thoughtfully.

Except Bella.

Bella threw her hands up in the air. "Am I the only one who can see this guy is an ass?"

"Bella. It's not your story," Kaitlin said gently and that shut Bella up. But, Emily suspected, not for long.

Tara shrugged. "You got a guy you really like who, according to some reports, can be an ass. But he's stepped up to the plate enough to apologize and ask for another chance—"

"You give him another chance," Kaitlin said.

Bella muttered under her breath.

"That's not the problem." Emily blushed. Now that she was having this conversation, she wished she'd never brought it up. How mortifying was it to ask your best friends how to seduce a man? She had no experience with men, save a hurried tryst involving a copious amount of maple syrup in a rustic cabin and some desperate fumbling in a glass studio. She had no idea how to proceed.

"What's the problem?"

Emily folded her fingers together. "He...wants to prove himself to me."

Kaitlin pursed her lips. "Prove himself?"

"He...um...wants us to take things...slow."

"Ah," Tara murmured. "The old Lysistrata."

"The old Whatsistrata?" Bella asked.

"No sex."

"No sex?" The others screeched.

Avery frowned. "We are talking about Ash *Bristol*, right?"

"He is very determined to be a perfect gentleman. And I...well...I..."

Mel winked. "You want a little something-something?"

"I just don't know how to show him I'm ready."

"You could just tell him you're ready." Tara suggested.

Emily pouted. "I tried. I don't think he believed me. So, what do you recommend guys?"

"Seduction." Tara offered gleefully.

"I'm hardly a seductress."

"I think you underestimate yourself," Kaitlin said with a smile.

Tara plucked a kitten from her shoulder. It immediately crawled back up. "Men are notoriously easy to seduce. All you have to do is wear sexy underwear."

"And give him a blowjob." This from Mel.

Avery nodded. "Better yet, give him a blowjob *in* sexy underwear…"

Emily tapped her lips as she considered these suggestions. She certainly wanted to try pleasuring Ash the way he'd pleasured her in the cabin. But thinking up things to do to Ash's body wasn't the issue. She was able to think those things up on her own. "What if he resists my advances?"

"He's not in his right mind."

Emily frowned at Avery. "Seriously. I need a plan."

"If he gets all chivalrous and shit, you need to tease him until he simply cannot resist," Mel advised.

"Wait," Jamie said. "Didn't he also offer you the opportunity to punish him?"

Avery sat up straighter. "Oh, do tell."

Emily flushed. She didn't want to make Ash suffer. It wasn't in her to punish anyone.

Tara cracked a mischievous grin. "So punish him."

"Now you're talkin'," Bella crowed. "Make him pay."

Tara glared her down. Tara hated being interrupted when she was hatching a vengeful plot. "Punish him in the worst way a woman can punish a man."

Jamie tipped her head to the side. "Talk during football?"

"Not heinous enough." Tara dumped a coterie of kittens off her lap and went to the table to refill her wineglass. She waggled the bottle at Emily. "Are you sure you don't want some wine?"

Emily and Kaitlin shared a glance. Emily shook her head. "No. I… My stomach's been upset lately."

Tara shrugged and upended the bottle. "So, let's see…how can we punish Mr. Ash Bristol?"

"You should punish him…*sexually.*"

Emily's pulse stuttered. She gaped at Mel. "I-I couldn't."

"Oh, yes you could." Tara chuckled. She turned to Avery, seeking support. Which she found. They were both devious to the extreme.

Avery stood too, and began pacing the room. Always a bad sign. "You really want this guy?"

Emily swallowed. "Yes."

"You want him to really really want you?"

"Y-yes."

"You want to make him crazy? So he can think of nothing and no one but you?"

"Um...yes?"

"Do you want him on his knees before you begging?"

Oh dear. That was going a tad too far. "I just want him, Avery. That's all."

A glint shone in Avery's wide, innocent, baby-blue eyes. They were misleading, those eyes. Avery was a man-eater, plain and simple.

"Trust me, honey," she said. "If you follow my plan, that boy won't know what hit him."

CHAPTER FIFTEEN

To Ash's surprise, on Monday Emily called him up and asked him out for their next date. It excited him, because it meant, perhaps, he was making headway in his wooing. If she was engaged in their relationship enough to plan a date, that meant she was seriously considering forgiving him.

He smiled to himself as he drove over to her house, wondering what kind of date she might plan. Something romantic and sweet, probably. A ride on the Ducks. A tour of the Seattle Underground. A dinner cruise… He scuttled that idea. Dinner cruises were expensive and she was a teacher.

Bowling maybe?

She met him at the door looking beautiful in a black cocktail dress and shiny pumps. He swallowed the drool collecting in his mouth and handed her the daisies he'd brought and leaned in to kiss her cheek.

Probably not bowling, based on the way she was dressed.

Curiosity rose, but was quickly overwhelmed by something else entirely. When she set her hand on his chest, gently, like a kitten, his pulse set up a manic tattoo. As she moved closer and closer still, her scent, her perfume, wafted toward him, enveloped him. Made him dizzy.

He drew in a breath, bringing with it her essence. God, she was beautiful. Tantalizing. Irresistible.

Had he really agreed to no sex?

What had he been thinking?

She put her hand on his nape and went up on her toes. Her lips parted. He ached to taste her. Couldn't wait. He dipped his head so she wouldn't have to stretch so far and—

Their lips met.

Electricity sizzled through him.

He'd never had a kiss that tasted this sweet.

Soft and supple, fragrant, sublime. Her mouth was a haven. He wanted to sink into her and stay there forever.

Fortunately, she did not seem inclined to end the innocent kiss.

He let her take the lead. He owed her. At least this much.

Torture though it was.

He longed to pull her close, deepen the kiss. Ravage her.

She deserved to be the one in power in this relationship. He just hadn't realized how much it would cost him. She set her palm to his cheek and cradled him, tipping her head slightly to the side and—Jesus Mary and Joseph—dabbed her tongue into his mouth.

Holy God.

It took everything in him not to yank her against him, walk her over to the wall and grind himself to heaven. He fisted his hands, steeled his muscles and allowed her to continue her exploration. Which, to his utter dismay, took her over his chin and down to the crook of his neck. He shivered and shook in utter agony as her sweet lips nibbled and nipped. A suck here a lap there. A low moan.

His cock, already unruly and rampant, screamed for attention. It was a heavy weight between his legs, throbbing and aching and hungry for her touch.

But even now, even as adrift as he was, Ash knew, if she touched him there, he'd be lost.

He was an honorable man—when he chose to be. And he had given her his word. No sex until he'd earned her trust.

What the fuck had he been thinking?

She wrapped her arms around his neck and cuddled up against him, rubbing him in just the right way. He gritted his teeth and shut his eyes, trying to focus on keeping his hands to himself.

When she pulled away, something inside him wilted.

God, he wanted her.

"Are you ready for our mystery date?"

"And how. Where are we going?" he asked as he held the door for her.

Her wicked expression shocked him to the core. "We're staying here."

Gooseflesh prickled on his nape. He blinked at her. Several times. "Alone?" Was that a hint of panic in his voice? Definitely. Panic.

He didn't think he could do that. Be alone with her and keep his hands to himself. It had been way too long since he'd had her.

A month was far too long.

He was weak. Vulnerable.

Hungry.

"Emily, I don't think you understand—"

She cut him off. "Did you mean what you said? About making it up to me?"

"I did. I've been trying…" But hell. How was he supposed to control himself in her living room? Her kitchen? Her freaking foyer?

Doubt flickered over her expression. He hated it, so he forced a smile. "Yes. Yes. Emily. I meant it."

"Anything I want?"

He gulped. "Anything."

Her response was a gamine grin. How a woman with such a sweet innocent mien could appear so evil was beyond him.

"Then we're having dinner here."

His heart ker-chunked. They were utterly alone.

And they would not be disturbed.

Holt would not be glaring at them from across the room.

There would be no crowds to shoulder through. No waiters or waitresses to interrupt with an offer of coffee.

How on earth was he going to survive this?

He swallowed heavily. And nodded. "Okay."

As she showed him into the dining room, where an elegant, romantic, table was set, he took in the details of her home. While it wasn't a large house, it was perched on a hill overlooking Seattle. The décor was classy, elegant, simple. Chopin played in the background, masking the muted barking of her neighbor's dogs.

The view from her bay window was stunning, the city lights reflecting off the waters of the Sound.

It was so…*her*.

Perfect for a girl who liked to stare at water.

Despite his trepidation, dinner was delightful. They talked and laughed through the meal, both of them completely at ease. Well, perhaps not completely.

Every once in a while he would remember how alone they were. How close she was, how very eager she was, the lilt of her eyes when she came…and a simmering unrest would ferment in his bowels.

She seemed similarly effected…every once in a while. She would shoot him a glance and a flush would creep up her cheeks and she would lower her lashes and nibble her lower lip and, occasionally, lace her fingers together. He assumed it was nervousness.

Hell, he was nervous.

He didn't seem to have any trouble devouring the meal though, a delicious standing roast with Yorkshire Pudding. And then she brought out an incredible burnt crème. If he hadn't thought her the perfect woman before, he surely did now.

When he'd finished the last bite, he tossed his napkin on the table, gusted a sigh and looked at her. And froze.

Her expression made him restless.

"Emily?"

"Did you enjoy your dinner, Ash?" A shy smile.

"Yes."

"Are you ready for…dessert?"

He glanced at the burnt crème. Or what remained of the custard he'd inhaled.

"I…ah… Yes?"

A flush crept up her cheeks. Her lashes fluttered. She cleared her throat. "Good. Because there is…something I'd like to try."

The tone of her voice set his nerves humming.

"Wh-what is it?"

"Do you trust me?"

He stared at her. Did he trust her? Yes. But she was a woman scorned. God only knew what she had in mind. And he had invited her to punish him…

Hell. It didn't matter, did it? He'd agree to anything she offered. Anything at all to be with her.

"Yes."

"Excellent." The glint in her eye sent a raging wildfire through him. And then his heart skittered to a halt. Because she pulled out a pair of handcuffs.

Oh, they were covered with fur and all pink and shit, but they scared him to death.

Holy God.

His pulse pounded. Sweat beaded his brow. His cock rose.

"What-what are those for?"

"I think you know."

Shit. He did.

He wasn't sure if he should be excited as hell—or run.

"I've decided on the punishment you keep suggesting."

He watched in stunned silence as she dragged a chair to the middle of the room and waved toward it. "Sit."

Damn. That tone…

He'd never, in a million years, ever imagined Emily as a Domme, but that tone was definitely intransigent. He reminded himself that she was a teacher. And teachers were proficient at intransigent tones. And probably punishment.

"Emily…"

She shot him a look. And fuck. There it was again, that flicker of self doubt, a painful fragility. He never wanted to see that on her face. Ever. Instinctively he knew if he passed on whatever she had in mind, if he denied this chance with her, there would never be another.

And that was not acceptable.

So he crossed the room. And sat. He watched her warily as she circled him.

"Hands behind your back."

"Emily…"

"Hush now, Ash. You promised."

He bit his tongue. And put his arms behind the back of the chair, trying very hard not to wince as the handcuffs clicked shut around his wrists. He couldn't resist testing them. Yeah. They were tight.

"Where did you get these?"

"Avery lent them to me."

"Avery Warner?" He gulped.

"Mmm hmm." She traced his shoulder. A shiver walked up his spine.

"How-how do you know Avery?" He'd been to several of Avery's parties. Wild didn't begin to describe them.

"Avery and I are old friends."

She came around and stood before him. He felt vulnerable and warm and very, very aroused. He hadn't had a release in a month—he'd been holding out for her—and the need for it clawed at him. It occurred to him, just then, how idiotic his vow of complete abstinence had been.

It didn't help that he was handcuffed to a chair in Emily's living room.

She trailed her fingers over his cheek, his neck, his shoulder. And then she stepped back and reached behind her and— Oh. God. *Unzipped her dress.*

He drooled as she shimmied out of the back sheath to reveal the most incredible breasts, encased in black lace. He nearly swallowed his tongue as the dress slipped further down to expose a garter belt, holding up fishnet stockings, and black panties.

"I…gah." It was all he could manage.

She was, in a word, magnificent.

She kicked the dress away and stood before him in the sexiest outfit he'd ever seen. All that, and shiny black heels… His brain short-circuited.

His cock did not. It stood, stiff as a pike. Aching.

"I've been wondering…" she said.

"Hmm?" It took some effort to make his voice function. To come up with a word that cogent.

"Is this the punishment you had in mind?"

She cupped him as the words eased out. Ran her hand over his flank and across his hip and straight to his groin. And cupped him.

He nearly came out of his skin.

Shit.

Yeah.

Punishment.

"Emily…"

"Now now, Ash." She drew back, but only enough to peer down at him. "You were going to let me use you, weren't you?"

He gaped at her. "Use-use me?" Surely she hadn't been serious about that?

Her expression made his pulse hiccup. Oh hell. She was. She was serious.

She cradled her breasts and smiled at him and he nearly swooned. He tugged at his bound wrists. Damn, he wanted to touch her, hold her, thumb that pouty nipple just visible through the lace.

"You know, Ash, there's something I've wanted to try, ever since that morning at the cabin…"

She left the room and he tracked her frantically with his gaze. *Where was she going? Leaving him alone? Bound to a chair?* Maybe these were trick handcuffs… He fiddled with them, turning his wrists this way and that. But no. Damn it. They were real handcuffs. No release—

She returned carrying something. He froze when he recognized it.

"Do you like chocolate syrup?" she asked playfully, waggling the bottle.

"I-yes."

"Excellent. Me too."

His vision narrowed to a tight point when she knelt before him, slid a palm up his thigh and toyed with the hook on his slacks. When her hand brushed against his cock, he threw his head back and groaned.

She ignored him and focused on her task. Her tiny pink tongue peeped out. It drove him wild. Unzipping his slacks, she opened the placket, and looked up at him with a mischievous glint in her eye.

"Emily…"

She tugged down his briefs and his cock sprang free. She stared at it. Gulped. And damn if she didn't lick her lips.

He nearly came right then.

"Emily…"

She picked up the bottle, merciless witch that she was, and drizzled chocolate all over his aching rod. He nearly went through the roof.

"Damn," he squawked. "That's cold."

"Sorry," she said. But she wasn't. "Let me warm it up."

He writhed in his seat as she did just that, spreading the sticky syrup all over his cock, fisting him, stroking him, smearing him with her special brand of sweet torment.

"Oh. I do believe I made a mess," she cooed. He glanced down. Chocolate stained his best slacks. He couldn't have cared less. All he saw was her fist circling his cock. The sight sent a vicious snarl of lust through to his solar plexus. He yanked at his bonds.

One would think, at such a moment, one would have superpowers. At the very least, powers strong enough to break the fuzzy pink hold on his wrists.

One would be wrong.

She shot him an innocent look, all pouty and fiendish. "I guess I'll have to clean it up."

"Em—"

She didn't give him time to protest. She went up on her knees and tightened her hold, drawing his cock toward her tantalizing lips. She pumped him a time or two, with her breath hovering there, holding him on the knife's edge of anticipation.

And then she licked him.

He might have passed out. Just for a second. So sharp was the pleasure.

"Emily." A plea.

"Mmm," she murmured. "I do love chocolate." And she proceeded to prove it. Licking and lapping and sucking along the length of his cock. Tormenting him, teasing him, making him squirm and growl and then, eventually whimper.

And then, when he didn't think he could bear it any longer, she levered up, changing her angle. He dared not move, hoping, dreading, desperate for…

Ah.

God.

Yes.

She came down on him, sucking him in. Suckling him. Nibbling. And then deeper and deeper still.

"Mmm." Her moan ricocheted through his body, an excruciating vibration.

She couldn't take him all in, so she took him as far as she could and stroked him at the base.

His life, his world, his sanity, shrank down to that point of contact, that sensation, that agony of want.

He screwed his eyes shut, so he couldn't accidentally watch. Seeing his cock disappearing between those ruby red lips would surely send him over the edge and he didn't want to come. Not yet. Not now. Not like this.

He wanted to be in her. Come in her. Claim her. Take her.

He wanted to fuck her. Madly. Passionately. Wildly, as he had ached to do for far too long.

But she was ruthless, his mistress.

And, in her innocence, brutal.

She released him, but only to resume the agonizing licking and lapping. She was a diligent girl, his Emily. Determined to get every drop of that chocolate.

"You taste good," she said, sitting back on her haunches. Chocolate rimmed her mouth, smudged her cheeks.

"Come here."

But she didn't. She just laughed and upended the bottle again.

He winced as the cold chocolate dribbled up the length of his cock. She put an extra large dollop on the tip. And then, God help him, she sucked him in again. This time, dabbing her tongue into the little eye while she pumped him.

As if that wasn't enough, she stroked, cupped his balls, rolling them gently, smearing them with syrup.

That was what did it.

The thought, the vision, the fantasy of her tongue lapping at his balls, combined with the incredible sensations she was drawing in him, combined with the way her finger tickled one very sensitive spot down there—right where it counted—combined with the fact that he hadn't come in nearly a month…

He exploded.

It was a rapturous release, flooding through him in a torrent, rushing, screaming, howling relief and pleasure. Hot, jetting passion.

She took it all. Took it all in, and then lapped up the bits she'd missed, swirled as it was with chocolate.

He collapsed in on himself. Unable to move, to think, to react as she gently undid her dirty work.

He was still panting, groaning insensibly, when she unlocked the handcuffs.

As soon as he could move, think, function, he yanked her into his arms and kissed her. Not a sweet, adoring kiss as he had pressed on her earlier, but a feral, hungry, forceful kiss, laced with vicious need.

He wanted to fuck her. Claim her. Take her. But he was drained.

Not too quiescent though. Not so drained that a little maggot could not crawl into his brain and nest. He pulled back and frowned at her.

She set her palm on his cheek. The dampness told him he now had a chocolate handprint there.

"Ash? What's wrong? Didn't you like that?"

"Oh, I liked it, all right."

She blinked at his vehemence. "Then why are you angry?"

"I'm not angry."

"They why are you frowning?"

"Where did you learn that?"

Her brow knit. "What do you mean?"

"That," he flapped a hand toward the chair.

Emily paled. "I… Was it bad? Did I do something wrong? I should have known…" Tears welled in her enormous eyes. Ash's gut clenched. He pulled her back into his arms and cradled her.

"Oh, no. No. It wasn't bad, honey. No. Don't cry. It was…hell, it was awesome. It's just… Not very many women are that…creative."

"Creative?"

"Adventurous."

"Adventurous?" She cringed.

Shit.

"Experienced."

"Experienced?" She pulled back to frown at him.

Her expression sent a shiver of disquiet shimmying down his spine. "Why are you looking at me like that?"

"You're the only man I've ever…" She colored. "You know."

He gaped at her. "What? What did you say?"

"Which part?"

"I'm the only…" The only man. Her only. Ever?

"Yes, Ash." She tipped her head. "I thought you knew. I mean, when it's a woman's first time, doesn't a guy just know?"

He snorted a laugh. "The only thing a guy just knows is that it's a time. But shit. If I'd known…I would have made it better."

"It was fine."

"Shit." He slapped his forehead. She'd said that, hadn't she? *Please be gentle?* He hadn't made the connection. He was a moron.

"Ash. It was wonderful." She smiled at him and he became tangled in the web of her beauty, her innocence.

Something swelled and prickled in his chest. His heart, perhaps, coming back to life. The tender ache surprised him.

He was the only man she'd ever been with.

This perfect, darling, tantalizing creature dressed in black lace and heels and smeared with chocolate. She'd tied him up. And sucked him off. And damn. He wanted her.

He wanted her forever.

As incomprehensible as it was, his cock rose again.

"I want to make love to you," he said, kicking off his slacks.

She took a step back. "But I'm covered in chocolate."

"Perfect." A growl. "I want to make love to you in the shower."

He eased the strap of her bra off her shoulder and then the other, slowly revealing her. He stroked her breasts, thumbed her nipples and pinched them gently. Arousal rocketed through him.

"Strip," he muttered.

She quivered as she complied, kicking off her shoes and her stockings, the garter belt and her panties. Her bra. They all fell on the floor, forgotten. He stripped as well and met her in a full-bodied hug.

Heaven.

Holding her was heaven.

He skimmed his palm down her back, from her nape to the gentle curve of her bottom, then sank his fingers in deep. She sighed and wriggled against him. "Let's go to the bedroom," she whispered.

"Let's." But he had to kiss her first. Consume her.

She tasted like chocolate and Emily and sweet perfection.

He tightened his hold as heat rose between them. Deepened the kiss.

A soft thud and a faint clicking sound registered on his brain, but he didn't bother thinking about what it could be until something cold and wet touched his bare ass.

He squealed like a little girl and leaped back, grabbing a fuzzy pink pillow from the armchair to cover his naked crotch. He shot his gaze around the room and froze.

A herd of velociraptors regarded him curiously, heads cocked to the side.

No.

Not velociraptors.

Dogs.

And cats.

A lot of cats.

And kittens.

"Oh dear," Emily murmured. "They got out."

"Out?" he croaked.

She nodded and pulled on her dress and began collecting cats. "I put them in the spare bedroom while we were having dinner." She shot him a naughty grin. "Chocolate isn't good for dogs."

"I...ah...right." He followed her lead and pulled on his slacks. He felt too vulnerable, naked amidst her menagerie, with dogs eyeing him as though he were a flank steak.

"I should have known better. Li Shang is something of an escape artist." She carried a bundle of kittens to the spare bedroom and set them on the bed, but before she could close the door, two of the kittens scampered out. When she headed for the older cats, they hissed at her and slunk off into the shadows.

A three-legged dog snatched up one of his Ferragamos and danced around the room, dodging back and forth to avoid Ash's lunging grasp. A diminutive Yorkie, shaved bald in odd spots on his body, leaped up on the table and began licking the chocolate bottle.

"Oh, no!" Emily squealed. She dropped the cats she'd collected and ran to the table, snatched up the bottle and frowned at the Yorkie. "No no, Prince Phillip. This is not for dogs. It's for grownups."

And suddenly, Ash couldn't help it.

As frustrated as he was, as *horny* as he was, this was pretty damn funny. He burst out in peals of laughter.

Emily stared at him. Her lips twitched. Then curved. Then a giggle escaped. And a laugh. And a howl.

They laughed until tears streamed down their faces and laughed even harder when a couple of the dogs started playing tug of war with Emily's garter belt.

After she put the chocolate away, they sat together on the sofa, surrounded by fur balls, entrenched in tribbles. Just sat there. Together.

He tried to kiss her a couple times, but Beast, who was apparently very jealous, got it in his mind to join the party. Beast liked to French kiss and he didn't care whose mouth he got into.

That made them laugh too.

And it occurred to Ash, he hadn't laughed this hard in—he couldn't remember when.

He did finally get her into the bedroom. He had to bribe the dogs with the leftover roast and then stealthily sneak her back there when none of the cats were looking. But he did it.

And he made love to her, worshipped her. Explored and delighted every inch of her soft, sweet skin.

Before he levered over her and eased his aching cock home, he made it a point to bring her to orgasm, screaming orgasm, at least three times.

That he counted.

He woke her up to pleasure in the middle of the night, tormented her until she was writhing, groaning, gripping his hair. That orgasm was glorious...for both of them.

He would seduce her the next morning too, he vowed as sleep claimed him. But Li Shang escaped sometime in the night and released his fellow prisoners. When Ash awoke, it was to find the bed covered with snoring critters, lounging hither and yon. He cuddled Emily closer and smiled.

There was always the shower.

The cats probably wouldn't follow them in there.

CHAPTER SIXTEEN

The day of the big luau dawned bright and sunny, but Ash was in a dismal mood. He and Emily had come to the Island two days early to make all the final arrangements for their big event and had the extreme misfortune of running into her friends Drew Boone, Jamie Cook and Kaitlin Stringer on the ferry.

She'd invited them all to help with the fund-raiser so he should have expected them to be there.

What he hadn't expected was their assumption, nay, their insistence, that Emily stay at their place.

He'd loved the past few weeks, loved every minute of it, working with Emily on the coming fete. Working on something that mattered. In addition to pulling all the pieces together in record time, they'd had dinner each night, a plethora of coffee dates—with chaperones—and gone fishing together. Holt and Parker and Kaitlin had tagged along on that trip, but it had been fun nonetheless. And the excursion had gone a long way toward making peace with Holt. Fishing was legendary for male bonding.

Ash and Emily had even spent a bit of time in his studio, playing with glass. And contrary to her opinion, she did not make silly little art. Her pieces were damn beautiful. His favorite was the one they'd done together. Island Sunrise, an exquisite panel featuring their island.

Aside from all that, they'd enjoyed mind-blowing sex. And sleepy early morning sex and quick down and dirty sex. Ash had gotten used to waking up with her by his side. Kissing her good morning. Being the first thing she saw when she opened those beautiful clear blue eyes.

He'd even gotten used to sharing a bed with butt sniffers. Sort of.

The thought of sleeping alone palled.

So it was kind of annoying when they ran into her friends.

And said friends insisted she stay the weekend with *them*.

Though their house was next door, and it wasn't so very far away, it was too far by half.

To make matters worse, Drew had assumed the role of Emily's protector. Whenever Ash and Emily were together—setting up tables, carting supplies, coordinating the entertainment—Drew somehow magically appeared. And hovered. Clung. Like the third wheel he was. When Lane and Cam arrived to help out with the Friday night welcome dinner, he collected a couple more shadows.

Even though Emily had made it clear to them they'd worked things out, her friends weren't convinced. They watched him like a hawk.

As a result, Ash wasn't able to sneak so much as a kiss.

So when he awoke on Saturday, he was cranky.

He shuffled downstairs rubbing the sleep from his eyes and gratefully accepted a mug of steaming coffee from Parker, who had come to help with the event too. Ash hadn't slept much last night, and not just because he missed Emily. All the foster boys were staying in his rec room and they'd been up until the wee hours causing a ruckus, despite the valiant efforts of their chaperones to get them to sleep.

Likely no one had gotten much sleep last night.

Parker clapped him on the back. "You look like hell."

"Thanks."

"I…ah…" It was unlike Parker to stutter. That and his expression caught Ash's attention.

"What's up?"

Parker blushed. The scar on his neck went white. "I…ah…"

Ash chuckled. "You said that already."

"Shit, Ash." His friend scrubbed a palm over his broad face. "I just wanted to say thanks."

"Thanks?"

"For doing this."

Ash stilled as Parker's meaning hit home. He nodded. "Sure thing." He was doing this for Parker. And all the kids like Parker who, through no fault of their own, ended up in hell. They deserved better.

"You know I love you, man," Ash said. His voice broke on the words. Words he rarely said. But he meant them. A lot.

"Yeah." They shared a half-hug. A man hug. The way bros do. "I guess you're not a total jerk."

Ash grinned.

Thunder rose as a stampede of rambunctious boys—who apparently didn't need any sleep to create utter havoc—pounded up the stairs from the basement and burst into the great room amidst whoops and hollers. For them, field trips like this rarely, if ever, happened. They were abuzz with excitement. Today there would be boating, swimming, games and, if things went well, mentors.

A mentor for each of these wayward souls.

Ash was determined to make it happen.

"Are you ready for this fresh hell?" he asked.

Parker snorted. "Bring it on, baby. Bring it on."

Ash drew in a deep breath and gazed out over the lawn. The luau was a huge success. Tiki torches burned along the beach and the smell of barbecue rode richly on the breeze. The evening was cool and clear. Stars sparkled in the sky and the sounds of music and laughter tangled with the low thrum of conversations.

All of the special guests Emily had invited had come, and they were enjoying the event to the utmost. As Emily had planned, they'd all had a day filled with fun, interacting with the foster kids, playing balloon volleyball, competing in sack races and battling out a tug-of-war in the sand.

The kids had all been on their best behavior—there had only been one "accidental" fire—and it seemed as though most of them had found a mentor. Now they sat around in clumps, feasting to the gills, groups of wealthy socialites and business people, each chatting with one or two of the foster kids. Bonding.

He glanced at Parker, sitting against a pine on the tree line talking to a young boy. From their expressions, Ash knew his friend was sharing his story. Parker rarely talked about his past. And for good reason. But how powerful would it be for a kid who had been through similar horrors, to discover that a different kind of life, a successful life, was possible?

And how rewarding was it to be a part of making this happen?

A funny lump lodged in Ash's throat.

He loved this, he realized. Loved doing something that made a difference.

He'd taken on this fund-raiser as an excuse to spend time with Emily, never expecting *this*.

That through his journey, he would discover his purpose.

"Hi there."

A warm presence registered at his side. Without looking away from the panorama before him, he looped an arm around Emily's shoulder and pulled her closer. Kissed her forehead.

"How are you doing?" she asked.

"The event is a smash."

"I knew it would be."

"How could it not be? With you in charge?"

"It's been fun, but I've missed you."

He looked at her then, took in her adoring eyes, her bright smile. "I missed you too." A whisper. God, she was beautiful.

She was everything.

A tender ache rose in his chest.

He loved her, this bright, beautiful spirit. He loved her so much it hurt.

The thought should frighten him.

It did not.

Instead, it filled him with a dizzying hope, a fierce satisfaction. Peace.

Had it only been six weeks since he'd met her on the beach? It seemed like a lifetime ago.

"Oh, look," she cried. He tried not to be annoyed that something had stolen her attention. He followed her gaze and his heart swelled at the sight of Dad and Michelle making their way down the beach. Sam skipped along beside them, throwing rocks into the surf.

"They came," he breathed. Dad was doing much better, following doctor's orders and slowing down at work. Though Ash had made it a point to invite them, they hadn't known if they'd be able to make it out.

He and Emily strolled over to meet them and to his surprise, his father greeted her with a big hug. "Emily," he boomed. "As always, an excellent event."

"Thank you, Adam." She dipped her chin to hide her blush.

"And Ash. Son." Dad put out a hand and they shook. Then he pulled him into a hug. "I am so proud of you for doing this."

It was Ash's turn to blush. "It was all Emily's idea," he said.

"But Ash picked the charity," she put in.

Dad winked. "It's a damn good charity," he said. "One of my favorites." He sketched a wave at Parker, who waved back.

"Sorry we're late. Michelle...wasn't feeling well so we had to take the later ferry."

Michelle laughed. "And then I got sick again on the ferry. All that heaving."

Ash chuckled. "Must be rough seas. Emily got sick on the ferry too." He glanced at her in time to see her flush and nibble her lip and he realized he probably shouldn't have shared that. Her stomach had been bothering her lately and her nausea seemed to embarrass her. "Anyway. I am glad you're here."

"The event's going beautifully." Emily's voice took on a businesslike tone. "We've had record donations and most of the kids have new mentors." She smiled slyly. "But there may be a few more who could use a hand up..."

Adam chuckled. "Relentless as ever, aren't you, Emily?"

She bit back a grin. "Yes."

As Ash watched them interact, his suspicion solidified. Clearly, this wasn't the first time they'd met. Which surprised him. "So...um... You two know each other?"

Emily patted Adam's arm. "We've known each other my whole life."

"Really?" How had he only just met her? He shot an accusing look at his dad.

"Emily's father and I have been friends for years. You've met him, Ash."

Ash blinked. "I have?"

"Caesar? Caesar Donahue?"

Caesar Donahue?

Caesar Donahue was Emily's father? Shock, utter and complete shock, rocketed through him.

No wonder Lane had laughed when he'd so magnanimously announced he didn't care that Emily was poor.

Because she wasn't.

Not by a long shot.

Shit, next to her father, his was a pauper.

Emily had mentioned her father was scary. That was an understatement.

"Are your parents here, Emily?" Michelle asked.

"Oh no," she responded. "They're summering in the South of France."

"Oh." A coo from Michelle. "Nice is nice."

Emily nodded. "It is."

Ash gaped at her throughout this exchange, desperately trying to process this revelation. "But..." he sputtered. "You're a teacher." Okay. A ridiculous thing to say, and he hated the way it came out, as though he was accusing her of something.

But she just smiled. "Of course I'm a teacher. I..." A charming flush stole over her cheeks. "I love children."

He gazed at her, entranced by her. Ensnared. She would be a wonderful mother. She would make beautiful babies.

He was suddenly possessed of the urge to make one. Right now.

But this was hardly the time.

Because the sky exploded. All the guests turned to watch as fireworks lit the heavens, children and adults alike ooing and awing at the panoply of color.

And because they were all distracted, and because no one was looking— most especially Lane or Drew or, for heaven's sake, his father—Ash pulled Emily into his arms and he kissed her.

But good.

"Oh Ash," she murmured against his lips. "I have missed you."

"I've missed you too. How long do you think it will take before your protectors will trust me to be alone with you?"

She laughed. "They aren't very forgiving."

"Let's sneak away..."

"I can't leave." A wail. "It's my event."

"It's going perfectly."

"Where would we go? Your house will be crawling with boys and ours is full to the brim with girls. There will be no privacy…"

He pulled her closer. "Let's go to the island."

"Silly. We're on the island." She tipped her head to the side. "How much champagne have you had?"

"I didn't have any champagne." He grinned. "I mean *our* island. Where it all started."

She made a face. "That cabin is too rustic."

"It's remote." He kissed her nose. "That would be the point." He dropped a kiss on her forehead, her cheek. "I'll make the pancakes this time…"

With a bribe like that, how could she resist?

Ash stretched and stared at Emily as she came back to the bed. She paused to gaze at the glasswork he'd brought over earlier and set on the mantel, the piece they'd made together. Sunrise over their island. A forever reminder that this was their place. The muted fingers of dawn traced the panel, making it come alive.

A smile tweaked her lips. When she turned it on him, his heart melted.

He opened his arms and folded her into his embrace as she slipped back into bed. "Everything okay?" he asked, kissing her forehead. She nodded, although, for some reason he didn't believe her. He'd heard the noises in the bathroom, and she smelled of mint, as though she'd just brushed her teeth. Like six times. She curled against him. He tightened his hold.

She peeped up at him. He kissed her. Couldn't resist.

A frown flickered over her features.

"What is it, Em?"

"I, ah, have something to ask you." She shook her head. "No tell you."

Concern skirled through him. Something in her tone set his teeth on edge.

"I've been kind of sick lately."

"Yeah?" He'd noticed. But surely it was only the flu. Surely it wasn't something serious…

Her expression shifted. A flicker of fear. A hint of apprehension.

Oh. God. The sinking feeling in his belly returned, the one he'd felt as he'd waited in the hospital for news on his father.

What if it were something serious?

He couldn't bear the thought of losing Emily. She meant too much to him.

She'd become his everything.

She wiggled out of his hold and sat up next to him, folding her hands in her lap. He recognized that sign. A block of ice formed in his chest. "I went to the doctor."

He sat up too. "And? What is it?"

"I don't know how to say it."

"Just say it."

She glanced at him. Her eyes, so blue, so beautiful, so pained. It nearly killed him.

"What." A croak. "Em?"

"I'm pregnant."

His jaw dropped. "What?"

"It's okay. I'm not expecting anything of you. I'm not. But you deserve to know."

Something tender and necessary dribbled through his chest. A baby? A little Ash? Or an Emily with that incredible button nose? "Is it...mine?" he blurted, then winced.

She smacked him on the shoulder. "Of course it's yours, doofus."

Ah yes, he reminded himself. He was her only.

Even now, the thought sent warmth curling through him. An immeasurable comfort. He kissed her, slowly, reverently.

She pulled away with a laugh. "What was that for?"

"For picking me to be your first." He kissed her again. "Thank you for that."

"Thank *you*." She grinned. "It was a wonderful one night stand, by the way."

"Was it?"

"Yes."

"Not very effective, though. As a one night stand."

It'd been a string of one nights—each better than the last.

If he had his way, it would be a lifetime of them.

One night stands.

Every night.

For the rest of their lives.

She folded her hands. "So..." She cleared her throat. "What do you think? About the baby?"

"Darling." He pulled her back into his arms and showed her. Or tried to show her. But again, she pushed him away.

"Are you happy?" she asked. Apparently actions didn't speak louder than words. At least not where Emily was concerned.

"Very happy. Extremely happy. Insanely happy."

"Are you sure?"

He laughed. "I'm really sure. Emily, I couldn't be more delighted."

"Oh, Ash..."

"My father will be delighted as well."

"I am so glad for that," she grinned.

"I have something to tell you too," he said.

"What's that?" she quipped, clearly not anticipating the depth of his announcement. Certainly not as profound as hers, but still.

"I love you, Emily Donahue. I love you with every fiber of my being."

Her lips parted and a sigh gusted out.

But she didn't respond.

His heart pounded. His throat ached. Every muscle vibrated.

Silence stretched as she stared at him, stretched so thin it seared his nerves.

"Emily?"

His woeful prompt nudged her from her stupor.

"Oh Ash." She set a palm on his cheek. "Oh Ash."

She didn't say the words. She didn't need to. He could see her love shining in her eyes and he knew.

Just knew.

He reached over into the drawer in the bedside table and pulled out the small box he'd hidden there. A box filled with something sparkly.

And he opened it.

AN EXCERPT FROM

DEVLIN'S DARE
Book 5 in the Tryst Island Series

"*That's* Devlin Fox?"

Tara stared at the group of guys carousing at the table on the other side of the bar. It wasn't bad enough that the gorgeous guy she ran into on the ferry turned out to be friends with the douche in the ascot she'd been running from. No.

He had to be her worst enemy too.

Damn. Damn, damn.

"You know him?" Bella asked.

"He writes a Foodie Blog." She glared around the table. "He gave Stud Muffin a bad review."

"What?"

"Why did he do that?"

She crossed her arms over her chest. She'd spent her life learning her craft. Spent her life savings opening her own bakery. Spent years building clientele. And then, with one crappy review, business had tanked. It was unfair for one man to have so much power. "Because I don't have gluten free." And then, under her breath, "Big baby."

Still, gluten free was a big deal in Seattle. She'd spent the past week working up recipes.

"What are you thinking?" Kaitlin asked in a whisper.

Tara froze. It didn't do to *think* around Kaitlin. Not that she read minds, or at least she insisted she didn't. But she seemed to *know* things regardless.

"Nothing."

Kaitlin's face rumpled, as though she smelled something nasty. Like a lie.

But hell. Tara couldn't tell Kaitlin what she was really thinking about because Kaitlin—the sweet, innocent soul she was—would try to talk her out of it. Ramble on about Karma and shit.

No, Tara couldn't tell anyone what she was really thinking about.

Because she was plotting revenge.

She was going to get Devlin Fox back. And she was going to get him good.

"Hi there."

Devlin turned on the barstool, his trademark smile plastered on his face. Everything within him froze. It was her. That little slice of heaven from the ferry. Damn. She was just as hot as he remembered.

She sidled up next to him. Interest—and something else—rose.

"Well hello there."

He liked her scent, something floral and light. He liked her heat as she pressed against his side. She lowered her long lush lashes and peeped up at him through the fringe. Damn, that was sexy. She licked her lips. That was sexy too.

"I never got to thank you," she purred.

"Th-Thank me?" Was that her hand? On his thigh?

Shit yeah.

"For saving me." She smiled. Her fingers flexed. "I would have tumbled to my death if you hadn't grabbed me."

"I doubt you would have tumbled to your death. Disfigurement, perhaps. Dire injury. But not death. Don't exaggerate."

She laughed, a low chortle. "Still. Thank you." She leaned closer and whispered, "Can I buy you a drink?"

Devlin blinked. He'd been hit on in bars before, but no woman had ever offered to buy him a drink.

She might just be a perfect woman. "Sure."

"What's your poison?"

"Whiskey sour."

She signaled to the bartender.

"So…I'm Devlin."

"Devlin." She cooed. Actually cooed.

"And you are…?"

"Interested."

He jumped a little as her hand skated up his thigh. His pulse skipped. "I…ah…yes. But what can I call you?" He had a pretty good idea where this was headed, and he wanted to know what to bleat as he sank into her steamy depths. It was only polite to know a woman's name at a moment

122

like that.

She pursed her lips, as though she were thinking it over. Or thinking about something else. Her thumb snaked up. Nudged his balls, just ever so lightly, and through thick denim, but he felt it like an electrical charge. "Call me Sugar."

"Sugar." Oh yeah. She was sweet. "Would you…like to go for a walk?"

"A walk?" His cock lurched.

"It's a beautiful night…"

She glanced over her shoulder and then threaded her fingers in his, leading him toward the back of the bar. He didn't know why they weren't heading for the front door, but didn't much care.

She was a beautiful woman. She wanted him. And he was just drunk enough to follow her anywhere she led.

He shot a glance at Parker who took in the scene in a glance and sent him a thumbs up.

They barely made it out the back door of the bar before she kissed him. Damn. Backed him up against the wall and threaded her fingers in his hair and pulled his head down and took his mouth.

And damn, she was a good kisser. She ate him with heat and passion and carnivorous zeal. He responded in kind, thrusting his tongue into her mouth. He nearly passed out when she sucked on it, nibbled it, toyed with it. He couldn't help imagining her doing the same to his cock.

Her palm roved over his chest and made its way down to his hips. His held his breath as she slowly teased the band of his jeans. She pulled back and held his gaze as she popped the snap.

"Mmm." She rumbled, reaching in. He hissed in a breath as she molded his length. Squeezed. "Such a big boy." She licked her lips and his brain short-circuited.

When she went to her knees before him and blew a hot breath on him through the cotton of his briefs, he nearly lost consciousness. "I want to suck you," she said. "Take off your pants."

Holy God. Yes.

In a frenzy, he kicked off his shoes, and ripped off his jeans, hopping from one foot to the other. He held still, frozen in place, as she hooked her thumbs in his briefs and eased them down. His cock sprang free. She dragged his underwear down until they pooled at his ankles.

He heard the catch of her breath. Felt the trace of a warm finger around his swollen head and down to the base. He shuddered.

"Ah. Yes," she said, coming close. Her breath skated over him. His knees knocked. She fisted him. Pumped. Once. Twice. Blood pounded at his temples. Thrummed in his cock. She bent closer. Her damp breath kissed the head. "Such a big dick," she said.

If he'd been in his right mind, her tone would have warned him, but he wasn't in his right mind. He was a little drunk and a lot horny and there was a gorgeous woman on her knees before him with his cock in her fist. And her mouth hovered just over the tip. Yes. Yes. Just a little more...

She released him and stood up in a rush. Her beautiful, seductive expression morphed into something bitter. He gaped at her, stunned.

"Yeah," she said, propping her fists on her hips. "You, Devlin Fox, are a big dick."

And then she whirled on her heel and left. Left him standing there, half-naked, leaning against the grimy brick wall behind a grungy little bar.

And she took his jeans.

ABOUT THE AUTHOR

Her Royal Hotness, Sabrina York, writes naked erotic fiction for fans who like it hot, hard and balls-to-the-wall, and erotic romance and fantasy for readers who prefer a slow burn to passion.

An award winning author of hot, humorous stories for smart and sexy readers, her titles range from sweet & sexy erotic romance to BDSM to erotic horror. Connect with her on twitter @sabrina_york, on Facebook or on Pintrest. Check out Sabrina's books and read an excerpt Amazon or wherever e-books are sold. Visit her webpage at www.sabrinayork.com to check out her books, excerpts and contests. Don't forget to enter to win the royal tiara!

BOOKS BY SABRINA YORK

Adam's Obsession (Erotic Contemporary, Ellora's Cave)
Dark Duke (Erotic Regency, Ellora's Cave)
Brigand (Erotic Regency, Ellora's Cave)
Dark Fancy (Erotic Regency, Ellora's Cave)
Dragonfly Kisses: A Tryst Island Erotic Romance (Erotic
Contemporary)
Extreme Couponing (Erotic Contemporary, Ellora's Cave)
Fierce (One Night Stand, Decadent Press)
Five Alarm Fire (Erotic Contemporary for the High Octane Heroes
Anthology, Cleis Press)
Folly (Erotic Regency, Ellora's Cave)
Lust Eternal (Erotic Fantasy, Ellora's Cave)
Pushing Her Buttons (Erotic Contemporary, Ellora's Cave)
Making Over Maris (Erotic Contemporary, Ellora's Cave)
Man Hungry (Erotic Contemporary, Ellora's Cave)
Rebound: A Tryst Island Erotic Romance (Erotic Contemporary)
Rising Green (Erotic Horror, Ellora's Cave)
Saving Charlotte (Erotic Contemporary for the
Smokin' Hot Firemen Anthology, Cleis Press)
Smoking Holt: A Tryst Island Erotic Romance (Erotic Contemporary)
Training Tess (Erotic Contemporary, Ellora's Cave)
Trickery (Erotic Contemporary with Magical Elements, Ellora's Cave)
Tristan's Temptation (Erotic Contemporary, Ellora's Cave)

www.ingramcontent.com/pod-product-compliance
Lightning Source LLC
Chambersburg PA
CBHW060626130626
46555CB00002B/684